When Megan heard the beep of Devin unlocking his car, she finally took notice of the car he was headed toward. Low-slung, sleek and red.

As he opened the door for her, she let out a low, appreciative whistle. "Nice car. Divorce does pay well, it seems."

"That it does," he answered, then closed the door on any further comment she might have made.

Devin braced his hand on the back of her seat as he backed out of the space, and she got an unwelcome reminder of why this was such a bad idea. He was only inches away, and even the tiniest movement of his hand would cause his fingers to brush against the nape of her neck. Goose bumps rose on her skin and she fought back a shiver. The tiny sports car meant his arm brushed hers as he shifted gears, and every time she inhaled the familiar scent of his aftershave tickled her nose.

She had to get control of herself. "A red sports car—aren't they supposed to be overcompensation devices for men who are, ahem, *lacking?*"

Dev's smile was wicked in the half light of the car, and she knew instantly she shouldn't have gone there. "I don't remember you complaining about my lack of anything. In fact, you seemed more than satisfied with my compensation."

KIMBERLEY LANG hid romance novels behind her textbooks in junior high, and even a master's program in English couldn't break her obsession with dashing heroes and happily ever after. A ballet dancer turned English teacher, Kimberly married an electrical engineer and turned her life into an ongoing episode of *When Dilbert Met Frasier.* She and her Darling Geek live in beautiful north Alabama with their Amazing Child—who, unfortunately, shows an aptitude for sports.

Visit Kimberly at www.booksbykimberly.com for the latest news—and don't forget to say hi while you're there!

GIRLS' GUIDE TO FLIRTING WITH DANGER

KIMBERLY LANG

~ THE EX FACTOR ~

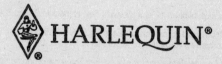

HARLEQUIN®

TORONTO • NEW YORK • LONDON
AMSTERDAM • PARIS • SYDNEY • HAMBURG
STOCKHOLM • ATHENS • TOKYO • MILAN • MADRID
PRAGUE • WARSAW • BUDAPEST • AUCKLAND

Rom
L

Recycling programs
for this product may
not exist in your area.

ISBN-13: 978-0-373-52808-0

GIRLS' GUIDE TO FLIRTING WITH DANGER

First North American Publication 2011

Copyright © 2011 by Kimberly Lang

To Dee, who taught me how to plant flowers, flute a pie crust, and form proper jazz hands. Despite her best efforts, I do none of these things well. Thankfully, she loves me anyway.

CHAPTER ONE

FIFTY MINUTES COUNSELING Mr. and Mrs. Martin left Megan Lowe's head pounding. She needed to talk with Dr. Weiss about getting their meds adjusted, or else one of them would end up killing the other soon enough.

Megan made a few notes in their file while the session was still fresh in her mind, and added it to the stack in her in-box. She then went in search of aspirin.

Julie, another of the three interns who handled most of the actual counseling here at the Weiss Clinic, held the aspirin bottle in her direction as Megan pushed through the swinging door of the lounge.

"I heard that all the way in here. You should be getting combat pay."

Megan laughed as she opened a bottle of water and popped two pills gratefully. "Their volume is just set on eleven this week. I don't think there's any actual danger to anyone or anything—except my eardrums."

"A thousand years in grad school and you end up the equivalent of a referee for pro wrestling." Julie shook her head sadly.

"Only it doesn't pay as well."

Julie tapped the sheet of newspaper under her hand, calling attention to the full-page, full-color ad for Devin

Kenney's book. "Well, if you can't sort them out, at least you can recommend a good divorce attorney."

Megan felt her eye begin to twitch. "That is not funny, Julie. Not funny at all." Why couldn't Devin toil away in obscurity like everyone else? She'd fielded a bit of press interest last year when Devin's radio show, *Cover Your Assets,* had gone into syndication, but since his book of the same name had hit the top of every bestseller list, she'd felt like the most famous ex-wife in America. Or at least Chicago.

"Actually, it is kind of funny." Julie's smile wasn't in the least bit sympathetic. "And the irony is just delicious."

"Don't make me hate you. It's annoying, not ironic. Plus, it's ancient history." History that should have been lost in the mists of time, only Dev had to make it part of his career.

"A marriage counselor whose starter marriage left Devin Kenney so bitter he made it his life's work to get other people out of their marriages? Sorry, Megan, that's delicious. And newsworthy."

"You have a very liberal definition of news." Megan flipped the paper over so the ad no longer stared at her. "New topic. Did you get your grant paperwork in?"

She didn't miss the eye roll that accompanied Julie's dramatic sigh as Megan went to get her lunch from the fridge, but Julie did pick up the new topic, thank goodness. The amount of time she spent thinking about Devin these days simply wasn't good for her mental health, and talking about it wasn't going to help either. Strangling Devin for putting her in this position *might,* but that wasn't really an option. No matter how tempting the thought.

They were joined a minute later by Alice, the clinic's receptionist, who brought a stack of messages for them both. Megan flipped through the papers absently, until one caught her interest. "The Smiths canceled?" Allen and Melissa Smith were her most fanatical clients. They had a standing Monday appointment promptly at one o'clock. They never missed it. "Did they say why?"

Alice winced as she put her lunch in the microwave. "Yeah, they did."

There was that eye twitch again. She wasn't going to like this. "And?"

"They're very uncomfortable with the level of notoriety you've reached lately, especially since that blogger who's been lurking around here called them at home yesterday to ask about you."

"That guy identified and called one of my clients?" She caught Julie's shocked face out of the corner of her eye. "*Please* tell me you're kidding."

"I wish."

"Oh, my God. That's…that's…"

"An invasion of the Smiths' privacy and a black mark on the reputation of this clinic." Dr. Weiss—the Weiss of the Weiss Clinic—spoke from behind Megan, making her jump.

"Dr. Weiss, I'm *so* sorry. This is just insane."

"I agree." Dr. Weiss looked unperturbed and calm, but Megan knew that might just be her "counselor face." Dr. Weiss had been a therapist for more than thirty years; she wouldn't show surprise if Megan jumped up on the table and danced a naked cha-cha. At the moment Megan sincerely wished Dr. Weiss wasn't quite such a master of the poker face. It was simply impossible to tell how much trouble—if any—she was in at the moment. Strangling Devin was sounding better and better.

"I'm sure this will blow over soon. I'm just not that interesting, you know. And we all know how fickle people's interest can be," she finished with a lame attempt at humor.

"I'm glad to hear you feel that way, Megan." Dr. Weiss's voice was understanding and kind, but that didn't stop the sinking feeling in Megan's stomach. "I think you should take some time off until it does."

The sinking feeling became a twenty-story drop. "What?"

Dr. Weiss joined them at the table and sipped her coffee. "You have plenty of vacation time, and now might be a good time for you to take it."

"But my clients…"

"We can handle them for a couple of weeks."

"*Weeks?* Dr. Weiss, I know this isn't a great situation, but…"

"Megan, I will not have my clinic turned into a three-ring circus. And I will not have our clients embarrassed or inconvenienced."

She felt like a chastised child—which was probably exactly what Dr. Weiss was going for—and anger at Devin boiled in her stomach. Julie and Alice were feigning attention to their lunches, but she could feel their pity and it tossed fuel on that fire. She fiddled with a pencil, focusing on it as she forced herself to remain outwardly calm.

"I understand. I'll work with Alice to get everything rearranged after I finish with my anger-management group this afternoon.…" She trailed off as Dr. Weiss shook her head.

"I'll handle your group."

The pencil snapped.

Dr. Weiss's eyebrows went up. "Perhaps you might wish to join the group this afternoon."

"No." She forced her jaw to unclench and tried to smile. "It's okay. I'll start getting everything together. Alice, when you're finished with your lunch, will you have a few minutes to look at my schedule?"

Alice nodded, and Dr. Weiss looked pleased—or maybe not. It was very hard to tell.

"This isn't a punishment, Megan. As you say, this will die down soon, and you can work on those journal submissions while we wait for it to pass."

"That's a wonderful idea, Dr. Weiss." *And I'll get right on that, right* after *I kill Devin Kenney.*

Megan managed to walk out of the break room with some small measure of dignity, but she couldn't get her fists to unclench. Her nails were digging painfully into her palms by the time she made it back to her office and shut the door.

Trying to focus on something other than Devin, she checked her calendar and started pulling files and making notes for Julie and Nate, the other therapist, who'd been with a client and missed the fun. But she was sure he'd be brought up to speed about thirty seconds after his client left.

I'm not fired. I'm not being punished. This will blow over.

Damn Dev. How many more times would she have to reorganize her life because of him?

This will blow over soon enough.

She kept repeating that phrase until she heard the soft knock and looked up to see Julie and Alice tiptoeing in.

"We're so sorry," Julie said.

"There's nothing to be sorry about. This will pass."

Julie sat in the chair across from her desk as Alice took the files from Megan's hands. "We all know hate is a very negative emotion," Julie began, "but I think we'd all agree that it's not an inappropriate one in this situation."

"Thanks, Jules." She sighed. "You know, I've never hated anyone before in my entire life."

"Not even Devin?"

"Oddly enough, no." At Julie's obvious disbelief, she tried to explain. "It wasn't like that. I was bitter and angry and hurt, but I didn't hate him. I was disappointed, disillusioned, heartbroken…but it never crossed over into actual hate." She shrugged. "And then I moved on. Dev's obviously the one with lingering issues."

"Sounds like he could use a good therapist." Julie smirked. "Know any?"

"Sadly, I'm off the clock for the foreseeable future." She rested her head on her hands. "All that time patting myself on the back because I'd moved on. Now *I'm* angry. The man is dead meat if I ever get my hands on him. Like I could," she scoffed. "I'm sure he's unlisted these days, and I doubt his firm would let me in the front door."

"You could just go to his book signing, you know," Alice offered.

That caught her attention. "His book signing?"

Alice nodded. "There was an ad in the paper today. He's signing books downtown today from three to five."

"Really. Hmm." Devin was in town—not off doing the talk-show rounds in New York or L.A. "Interesting…"

"Megan…" Julie's voice held a warning tone. "Do *not* make this worse."

Megan was already running a search on Google for the bookstore. "How could it possibly be any worse? He's already destroying my career, my reputation, my *life*."

"Nothing's in complete ruins just yet. Let's not build a bonfire in the rubble prematurely."

"I'm a professional, Julie. I think I can confront my ex-husband in a positive, appropriate manner."

Julie snorted. "You really think that?"

Megan lifted her chin. "I do."

"You know that means you can't kill him, right? Or even throw a punch?"

She leaned back in her chair and closed her eyes. "Unfortunately, yes. But I've got to put a stop to this somehow. Before it gets any more out of hand."

"You, Devin Kenney, are a force of nature, my friend. Incredible. You need anything? Water? A soda? By the way, love the shirt. It looks great on you."

Devin wasn't even slightly bolstered by Manny Field's exuberance or insulted that Manny bolted off before those words were fully out of his mouth. It was just part of the job. Manny saw everything in terms of his 15 percent, and Devin knew he was the biggest cash cow in Manny's herd at the moment; therefore, he was worth milking. *And sucking up to, as well,* he thought darkly. But Manny was his agent, not his friend—the kowtowing notwithstanding— and as his agent, Manny had made Devin a hell of a lot of money.

And vice versa—hence the pandering.

The last person in line approached. He scrawled his name one more time and handed the book over with a nod, trying to ignore the overbright smile and overenhanced cleavage of the woman gushing at him. She looked as if she was in the market for a husband—not looking to leave one. Just as the feeling registered, her next words confirmed that hypothesis.

"You know, Mr. Kenney—or can I call you Devin?— even after my last divorce, which your book would have helped me considerably with, I still think I'm a bit of a romantic at heart." She smiled coyly and leaned forward, offering him another view right down the front of her blouse.

"What about you? Are you still looking for true, lasting love?"

His on-air persona of Bitter Divorced Guy helped—a little—to avoid situations like this, but some women saw that as a challenge instead.

"If I—or anyone else—really believed in true, lasting love, I'd be out of a job."

That should have shut her down midflirt, but instead she leaned closer and murmured huskily, "Maybe you haven't met the right woman yet."

Maybe Manny needs to get his ass back over here and run some interference. He heard the quiet whir of a camera and knew this woman and her breasts were about to make the front page of someone's blog. *Great.* He didn't want to insult a fan with his rebuff, but he didn't want to hear the next offer either. *Where the hell is Manny?*

He scanned the store until he found Manny engaged in a conversation with a small blonde. Her back was to him, so he couldn't see her face, but Manny certainly looked aggravated. The woman spoke animatedly, the motion causing a long ponytail to sway against her shoulders. She was casually dressed, the white T-shirt skimming over a lovely back and narrow waist before it disappeared into the waistband of faded jeans. Those jeans hugged her butt in a way that got his body's attention—much more so than the cleavage nearly under his nose.

The woman hitched a battered brown bag over her shoulder, and something about the movement seemed oddly familiar. A moment later she turned to look in his direction and pinned him with a stare.

Megan.

Aware she now had his attention, she turned to face him, crossed her arms over her chest and tilted her head to one side. As her weight shifted onto her back leg, two realizations hit him at once.

First, the years had been very, *very* good to her.

Second, she was madder than hell.

Manny tapped Megan on the shoulder. Old instinct kicked in, and he was on his feet before he knew it. Manny could be caustic and slice people apart with mere words, and from the look on his face, Megan was seconds from getting the full Manny treatment. He barely glanced at the woman in front of him as he stood. "Enjoy the book. Hope it helps next time."

The woman's sputter barely registered as he crossed the bookstore, dodging a table full of his books, and got closer to Megan. As he closed the distance, her blue eyes narrowed, but not before he saw the cold fire burning there.

So the anger was directed at him, personally. Interesting. He should let Manny handle it, but his conscience wouldn't let Megan's feelings be hurt like that. It would be letting a bully kick a puppy, and regardless of anything else, he couldn't let that happen.

Plus, he was too curious now to see what had brought Megan intentionally back into his universe after seven years.

The freshman fifteen she'd battled in college was long gone, bringing out her cheekbones and giving her a delicate look that was at odds with the angry jut of her chin. That T-shirt scooped low on her chest, snuggling tightly against the curves of her breasts—breasts that the position of her arms were pressing together and up as if they were begging for his attention.

As if she realized the direction of his thoughts, Megan shifted, bracing her hands on her hips and pressing her lips into a thin line. With her light blond hair, big blue eyes, tiny stature and ticked-off look, Megan resembled an angry Tinker Bell at the moment.

Manny stood behind her, still talking, but Megan didn't spare him a glance. Her eyes bored into his as he approached.

"Sorry, Devin, but this woman says—" Manny started.

He waved Manny silent. "Not a problem." Manny sputtered, and Megan seemed to be grinding her teeth. Aware of their audience, he turned on his best media-honed charm and smile. "Megan, this is a surprise. I'm flattered you'd come."

She shook her head. "Don't be. You're a dead man, Dev." Her voice was quiet, but the heat behind it was fierce.

Manny took a step back. "I'll get security."

"No need. This is Megan Lowe. My ex-wife."

Manny scowled at Megan. "You didn't mention that."

She rolled her eyes in response. "Could you excuse us for a minute? I need to talk to Devin. Privately," she forced out between gritted teeth.

Manny looked at him for confirmation, obviously still ready to get security to remove a half-crazy woman. It wouldn't be the first time. Devin nodded. "It's fine, Manny. Give us a minute. I'm sure Megan doesn't actually plan to attack me."

"Wanna bet?" she snapped.

"I'm sure you wouldn't want to make a scene in front of fifty people, would you?" he warned. Megan was fired up about something, but he didn't want this to make the papers.

She looked around, then blew out her breath in a long sigh. The most fake smile he'd ever seen crept over her face as she turned to Manny again. "Of course not. I just need a few minutes of Devin's time." The sugary sarcasm dripping off her words didn't bode well for whatever she needed those few minutes for.

Manny backed off a few steps, and Devin reached for Megan's elbow. She jerked away before he could touch her. Lord, she really was mad, but why had she decided to confront him *here?* Whatever bee was in her bonnet, the middle of a busy bookstore during one of his signings wasn't the place to discuss it. With a sigh he indicated the stockroom he'd been stashed in earlier before the signing began. "How about in there?"

Megan hitched her bag up again and squared her shoulders. She walked stiffly, that fake smile fixed on her face until the stockroom door swung shut behind them. Then she turned on him. "How *could* you, Dev?"

"How could I what? You'll need to be more specific."

Megan pulled a copy of his book out of her bag and tossed it at him. *"This."*

He caught it reflexively and looked at her. When she didn't elaborate, he prodded her. "Should I make it out to you, or is it a gift for a friend?"

"Neither." She snorted. "I've got your autograph already. On my divorce papers."

"Then what?" She didn't answer, but he could see the muscle in her jaw working. "Need some legal advice?"

She tilted her head, and the end of her ponytail fell to rest on the heaving swell of her breasts above the neckline of her shirt. A faint flush colored the skin there, barely noticeable in the dimness of the stockroom. "Actually, I could use some legal advice. What's the difference between slander and libel?"

He pulled his attention from her cleavage. "What?"

"How about defamation of character? Can I sue you for that?"

Meggie rarely made sense when she got good and mad,

but this seemed to be extreme, even for her. "Why don't you calm down and tell me—"

"Don't you dare patronize me, Devin Kenney. Your radio show was bad enough, but this book…"

Old habits warred with each other. Placate or fight back? "I don't think—"

"And therein lies the problem. Did you never once think that people *might* be interested in the ex-wife of America's most popular divorce attorney?" Megan began to pace, her hands moving agitatedly as she spoke. "That people *might* think that some of the things you mention on the radio or the stories in this book are based on your *personal* experience? Or that they might come looking for *me,* wanting dirt or backstory or something?"

Ah, unwanted notoriety. "You're all spun up because some tabloid wants you to dish the dirt on me?"

She crossed her arms on her chest again as she stared at him, eyes snapping. "Not just *some* tabloid. *All* the tabloids. All the cable news channels. Half a dozen talk shows and every damn blogger in the universe. Do you not keep up with your own press? Haven't you seen *my* name next to yours recently?"

He didn't keep up with his own press; he didn't have time. That's why he had Manny. And they'd be having a conversation about *that* later on. After he finished with Megan.

Her anger made a bit more sense now. Megan was so shy, the media hounds would be too much for her to deal with without major stress. Feeling a twinge of guilt that Megan had been pulled into this media circus at all, he reached for her arm out of habit, simply to calm her. When she stepped back, he remembered he didn't have the right to touch her anymore. He leaned back against a stack of boxes instead. "The fact we were married once is public record. I can't change that." She took a deep breath, and he held up a hand, trying to be diplomatic. "But I *am* sorry you're being bothered by the press. It'll blow over soon." Something about that phrase made her nostrils flare and the color in her cheeks deepen. "Feel free to milk this any way you want, though."

"I don't want to milk this. I want it to go *away*. My career may never recover as it is, but if this continues…"

He tried to follow the change in topic. "Your career?"

"I realize it was never high on your radar, but surely you remember I wanted one of those, too."

Oh, he remembered, all right. She'd moved to Albany and filed for divorce in pursuit of her precious career. The bitter taste of *that* memory settled on his tongue and made his next words sharper than intended. "I don't see how a little fame could have any detrimental effect on your career."

"I'm a therapist." He shrugged in question and Megan's jaw clenched again. "Primarily a *marriage* therapist," she managed to grit out.

He felt his eyebrows go up, and a small chuckle escaped before he could stop it.

Megan rolled her eyes and sighed. "Yes, yes, I'm aware of the irony. As are all the people contacting me about you. But I'm damn good at what I do. And I was building a nice client list and decent reputation. Until now."

"And?"

"Let's see. The press won't leave me alone. They call my office and my house at all hours. My email overflows, and one even tried to pose as a new client. I could handle that, but now my *clients* are being harassed by the press, which is a horrible invasion of their privacy, not to mention embarrassing for them and the clinic I work for. The speculation in the tabloids about our marriage makes me look like some kind of psychotic harpy, which tends to make people think twice about listening to my advice." She was pacing again, working that head of steam back up. "Oh, and there's the little issue of being placed on extended leave because all of this interferes with the entire clinic's ability to do business. So, thank you, Devin, for screwing up my life. Again."

That accusation rankled, but he wasn't going to argue who had screwed up whose life in the first place. He'd win that battle. But that was ancient history. He did feel slightly bad Megan was catching flak—and that he'd been unaware of any of it. Regardless of his reputation, he wasn't completely heartless. Even when it came to her. "I didn't know. I'll try to do some damage control, if you want. Make it clear that we were so long ago that nothing of us is part of the book."

Her shoulders dropped. "It's a start. But I doubt it will help."

Old frustration edged its way back in. "Then exactly what *do* you want me to do?"

The question hung between them in the dim stockroom, and Megan didn't have an answer.

Anger and indignation had brought her this far and now she regretted giving in to either emotion. So much for "positive confrontation." All those "I" statements—*I think, I feel*—she was *supposed* to use in this situation had evaporated under the heat of her emotions. Good God, if Dr. Weiss had heard that outburst… She cringed inwardly. She'd be sent back to Psych 101 to start over again. The outrage drained away, leaving her feeling hollow and foolish.

It was a familiar feeling. One she didn't like.

She just hadn't been properly mentally prepared to see

Devin again. Face-to-face, at least. She'd debated taking this internship simply because Devin was so famous, and she wasn't sure she wanted to be in the same town. But an internship at the Weiss Clinic was too prestigious to turn down over an ex-husband. Not in a town this size, where she was practically guaranteed to never run into him.

Then she'd moved here and his picture was all over town: on the sides of buses, on billboards, in magazines. Devin's I'm-up-to-something smile was *everywhere*. It was wreaking havoc on her psyche, but she'd learned how to ignore it—for the most part.

But all that practice hadn't prepared her to be in the same room with him. *Alone*. His long, lean body took up way too much space, and her nerve endings seemed to jump to high alert. Devin appeared to suck up all the available oxygen in the room, leaving her with nothing to breathe except the unique scent of him that she—and something inside her—recognized immediately. Those liquid brown eyes, the way his dark hair curled just slightly behind his ears… Those hands—oddly elegant for a man who oozed testosterone from every pore—brought visuals she didn't need right now.

It was terribly unfair to discover that after all these years Devin still had an effect on her—especially when she obviously had no effect on him at all. Her inner eighteen-year-old was stuttering and stammering just being this close to him, and it irritated her to no end.

And now she'd stormed in here and acted exactly like some kind of crazy ex. And considering how reasonable *he* was being… She wanted to go hide under a rock for the next five years or so. She might recover her pride and get over the embarrassment by then.

Devin repeated the question, and the exasperation in his tone drove home how ridiculous she was being.

I should have listened to Julie.

"Well, Meggie?"

You could start by not calling me Meggie. It caused another one of those heartbeat stutters and brought back memories she was doing her damnedest to suppress. But the question did deflate the last bit of the outrage that had sent her storming downtown to confront him. She sighed and dropped her shoulders in defeat. "I don't know. I guess that's all you *can* do. Eventually my fifteen minutes will be up, right?"

Biting her lip, she reached deep inside for a bit of the professional behavior she'd lost in her tirade. Without the anger and indignation fueling her, she felt foolish. And Dev's proximity was just too much. "I apologize. I shouldn't have come here in the first place, so I'll go now." A small laugh at the absurdity of the situation escaped her. "I won't say it was nice seeing you again, but at least I can offer you my congratulations on your success in person." There. She could end on a less embarrassing and slightly more mature note.

Dev nodded, but he had the oddest look on his face—rather as if he was concerned she wasn't all there mentally. She couldn't really blame him for that. "Bye, Dev. And good luck." She held out her hand.

Seeming surprised and not bothering to hide it, Devin took her offered hand. *Damn it.* His touch caused her fingers to tingle, and it took all she had not to jerk her hand away.

"You, too, Meggie."

Pulling herself together by force of will, she released his hand and refused to look back as she walked away. She pushed the door with a little too much force, causing it to swing wide. That annoying agent jumped back to avoid being hit.

"Eavesdropping? Really? Lovely."

Manny had the sense to look a little abashed at being caught, but then he shrugged and grinned. It was a fake, practiced grin, and she wasn't the least bit fooled by it. Or by the false friendliness that followed. "You know, you really shouldn't take any of this personally. It's just showbiz."

She pretended to think about that statement. "Showbiz. Yeah. Well, for those of us who didn't sign up for it, it sucks."

Much like her life at the moment.

CHAPTER TWO

TWENTY-FOUR HOURS under the covers and more ice cream than any adult should ever eat hadn't solved anything. Megan didn't feel better about any of it. And now her stomach hurt, as well.

She was tired of hiding in her apartment, mainly because seeing Devin had awakened every old repressed memory, causing her to relive their entire history. She was a complete mess now, thanks to him.

When the phone rang, *again,* she flipped back the quilt to check the number. No name. *Damn.* Not answering wasn't an option, since it could be a client calling. They all had her cell-phone number in case of an emergency. She mentally crossed her fingers, then immediately felt bad for hoping one of her clients was having an emergency.

"Dr. Lowe?"

"Speaking."

"My name is Kate Wilson. I'm a producer—"

She sighed. "No comment. Goodbye." The press was driving her crazy.

"Wait! Don't hang up, please." Something in the woman's voice caused her to pause. "I'm Devin Kenney's producer for *Cover Your Assets.*"

That's why the voice sounded vaguely familiar. She'd heard it on the radio the once or twice she'd tuned in to

Devin's show—strictly for research purposes, of course. "And I still have no comment."

It wasn't for lack of trying, though. She'd spent hours trying to come up with the perfect comment. One that would be pithy and quotable yet shut down any further questions. Sadly, such a comment did not exist.

"I understand your reluctance, but please hear me out. I'm not looking for a quote or a story." The woman laughed. "That's not my job."

Megan focused on the water stain on the ceiling and prayed for patience. "Ms. Wilson, I'm extremely busy today, so—"

"So I'll get to the point. I understand you're getting a lot of unwelcome attention from the media right now."

That was an understatement.

"I don't know how much you've dealt with the media in the past, but I do know one way to get this circus under control."

That would be too much to ask, especially since this woman worked for the media—and Devin. Therefore her offer to help sounded suspicious at best. "And that would be...?"

"You beat them to it. Put yourself out there in a way you can control."

"Ms. Wilson—"

"Call me Kate."

"Kate, I'm really not interested in doing interviews or anything of that nature."

"Exactly. That's why I think you should come on Devin's show."

What part of "no interviews" does this Kate not understand? "I'm sorry, what?"

Excitement oozed out of the woman's words. "You could tell your side with Devin right there to corroborate the truth of the stories. You could take questions, even, and end the speculation. If you show that you and Devin aren't on opposite sides—and that you two think it's a nonissue—that issue will no longer be interesting. Problem solved."

That sounded way too good to be true. Too easy. "What makes you think anyone would—"

"Dr. Lowe, you have to know the fact you're a marriage counselor and Devin is a divorce attorney is the stuff blogs eat up. It just feeds on itself, and the more that's not said about it just gives rise to more speculation."

"I am aware of that." *Blindingly aware,* she thought as her eye began to twitch again.

Kate seemed to miss the sarcasm. "Then come on the show tomorrow night. You and Devin can address this issue head-on. Get the truth out there and end everyone's curiosity."

It couldn't be that easy. Plus… "I've never done anything on the radio before."

"Don't worry about that. You have a great voice, and Devin and I can walk you through the specifics."

"I don't know. Maybe I should talk to Devin first." Oh, the thought made her stomach hurt again.

"It'll be great for Devin's ratings, too. I think a lot of folks will tune in to hear you two sort things out. And think, you could become the most popular marriage counselor in Chicago. It would probably increase your patient list."

Something didn't quite feel right. "Why didn't Devin call me himself with this grand idea?"

"He's in Atlanta today for a book signing and won't be back until tomorrow afternoon."

It was tempting. Very tempting. Except for the talking-to-Devin part. And the being-near-Devin part. That hadn't gone so well yesterday. She cringed again.

Kate did have a point about taking control instead of being pushed along. And wasn't she always telling her clients to act instead of react?

But the radio? Devin had a coast-to-coast audience. She wasn't the same wallflower she used to be, but still… Who *wouldn't* be nervous at the idea of being heard by that many people? The possibilities for humiliation were *huge*.

But if it went the way Kate seemed to think it would… Maybe she could shut this down before it got any bigger and get back to work. Put Devin out of her life once and for all.

"Dr. Lowe? If this is going to work, we need to jump on it now. Before it gets any bigger."

Megan took a deep breath. "Then I guess I'll come on the show."

"Wonderful! You'll need to be here by six so I can brief you. Do I need to send a car for you…?"

Kate rattled off questions and instructions, but Megan was questioning her sanity and barely heard them over the sound of her head gently banging against the headboard.

Devin made the mistake of heeding Megan's advice about reading his own press just as his flight began its descent into O'Hare. He put his seat and tray table in the upright position, stowed his electronics and changed to printed media to occupy the last few minutes of the flight.

There, on the front of the entertainment section, in type large enough to be read from Coach, was a promo for tonight's show.

And Megan's name was right next to his.

What the hell?

According to this, tonight's very special guest would be his ex-wife, Dr. Megan Lowe. His surprise at Megan's doctor title was quickly swamped by the news that she was coming on his show.

Whose bright idea was *that?*

He reached for his phone, only to remember he couldn't use it. Waving over the flight attendant, he asked, "How long until we land?"

"Hard to say, Mr. Kenney. There's a bit of a line and we're going to have to circle for a while. I'll let you know when we get an updated ETA, though."

He didn't know who to call first when they landed—Kate, Manny or Megan. Scratch Megan, since he didn't have her number. This stunt reeked of Manny's machinations, but Kate could've had a hand in it, as well. They were probably in collusion to drive him insane. Ratings and money: the two things Kate and Manny could be guaranteed to jump on any possibility of.

He shifted in his seat as the pilot announced the delay to the rest of the passengers.

How had they talked Megan into this idea? She had a fear of public speaking. She hated being the center of attention. Their small, family-only wedding hadn't been all about finances—Megan just couldn't face the idea of being the focus of that many people. She was an introvert, uncomfortable outside her zone.

That protective instinct that had appeared out of nowhere yesterday swooped back in again. The feeling was both familiar and odd at the same time. He'd been trapped by that feeling the very first time she'd turned those huge baby-blue eyes on him, awakening some caveman instinct to protect and shelter her from the big, bad world.

But it should be long gone by now, beaten down by the way she'd walked out on him, buried by her selfishness and immaturity....

There was the feeling he was used to getting on those

rare occasions Megan crossed his mind. That older instinct had just been shaken loose by the surprise at seeing her the other day. That twinge of guilt he'd felt at the bookstore had been easily tamped down, even as several tenacious reporters had questioned him about their marriage in interviews yesterday. He'd evaded the questions as much as possible.

Megan wasn't a part of his life. She needed to go back to whoever she was and whatever she did when not crashing his book signing. She certainly wasn't relevant to his career.

And he sure as *hell* didn't want her on his show.

No man should have to deal with his ex-wife on a national platform. What drugs were Manny and Kate on to even consider it?

He should fire both of them.

And he just might, if this plane ever hit the tarmac and he could use his phone.

The high-rise building that housed Broad Horizons Broadcasting looked like any other office building on the Chicago skyline. Megan wasn't sure what she'd expected when the shiny black town car had pulled up at her door earlier to ferry her downtown, but she didn't feel as if she'd been brought to a radio station. It looked rather more like an insurance company or something. She thanked her driver as he held her door, feeling a bit like a celebrity herself from his deferential treatment.

As she walked into the building and read the company listings on the wall, she stifled a laugh when she saw the building was, indeed, an insurance company. And an investment firm, a law firm and several other things on different floors. She signed in at the front desk, and the elderly security guard's eyebrows went up when he read her name and destination.

"You're not what I was expecting, Dr. Lowe."

She wasn't sure if that was a compliment or not. "You were expecting me?"

"Ms. Wilson told me to send you straight up to fifteen when you arrived."

Ms. Wilson. Kate. *Not Devin.* She still hadn't heard from him, although Kate had promised to pass along a message for him to call her. They went live on the air in less than an hour, and she'd like to talk to Devin before then. They needed ground rules, a plan of action.... And she needed to be sure she had worked past all those stammers Devin seemed to cause in her *before* she made a fool of herself on air.

The guard walked her to the elevator bank. "I have to release the floor for you. Otherwise you'll have to go to fourteen first." At her look, he elaborated. "It's a security measure for the hosts and their guests." He inserted a key, pressed the button and gave her a friendly smile as he stepped out and the doors closed. "Good luck."

"Thanks," she answered, but the doors were shut and the elevator lurched upward. Megan tried to tell herself that the sinking feeling in her stomach was caused by the swift ascent, but she wasn't a very good liar. Especially to herself.

When the elevator dinged and the doors opened, she stepped out carefully. Once again she hadn't been sure what to expect, but so far, Broad Horizons looked a lot like every other corporate-type office she'd ever seen—gray cubicles, fluorescent lighting, sturdy carpet and the faint lingering odor of coffee and microwave popcorn. Most of the cubicles were empty, and the quiet of the post-five-o'clock workday had already begun to settle.

She stood there, feeling rather foolish and unsure what to do.

"Dr. Lowe!"

She recognized the voice as Kate's and turned. Like everything else, Kate was completely *not* what Megan had expected. Tall and willowy with long black hair that curled in perfect unruliness around her shoulders, Kate looked like a supermodel. Someone that beautiful should be on TV, not hiding on the faceless radio.

At the very least, she should be sharing a couple of Dev's billboards.

Megan felt plain and frumpy—and rather underdressed in a simple skirt, tee and cardigan. Kate looked as if she belonged on a catwalk.

A perfect smile nearly blinded her as Kate extended her hand and introduced herself. "I'm so glad you're here, Dr. Lowe. Tonight's show is going to be fantastic."

I'd settle for not horrific. "Why don't you call me Megan?"

Kate nodded before she indicated Megan should follow her through the labyrinthine offices. She had to trot to keep up with Kate's longer strides.

"I have to admit, Kate, you're not how I pictured you." Realizing how that might sound, Megan tried to clarify. "Your voice, I mean. It seems like you'd be—" *Yikes. That sounds even worse.* "I mean…"

Kate laughed. "I understand. No one looks like you think they should once you've heard them on the radio." She shot Megan a sly smile. "Except for Devin, of course. People expect a panty-ripper when they hear his voice, and he doesn't disappoint."

"Excuse me, a what?"

"Panty-ripper. You know, the kind of man you'd rip your panties off for."

Megan stumbled slightly over her own feet. She couldn't quite argue with that statement, but she certainly wasn't going to agree out loud. Hell, she'd been guilty of some panty-ripping on more than one occasion.... She stopped that train of thought. *Ancient history.*

Kate continued talking, thankfully unaware of the heat stealing over Megan's face. "But that's the key to Devin's cross-demographic appeal. The men like his content, and the women like his package." She winked. "What's the saying? Men want to be him and the women just want him."

Did Kate want him? Was there something going on between Dev and his beautiful producer? Megan told herself it was strictly professional curiosity, but that didn't explain the little pang in her stomach. "So where is he? Did you give him my message?"

"Devin's plane was delayed and he's been frightfully busy all afternoon. He must not have had a chance to call. But you'll see him shortly." Kate held open a door for her. "We don't have a Green Room or anything, but you can hang out here for a few minutes and make yourself comfortable. I'll be back in a couple of minutes to start prepping you."

Prepping? That sounded as if something painful was coming. Megan wished she had a clue what went on at a radio station.

As the door closed, she realized Kate had left her in a break room. Table, fridge, couch, coffeepot—it could have been in any office anywhere, except for the pictures on the walls. She assumed many of them were on-air personalities, but she didn't recognize their faces. Except Devin's, of course. She did, however, recognize the people they posed with—sports stars, celebrities, politicians. Dear Lord, was that the vice president shaking Dev's hand?

The realization hit her a little too late. Some of America's most popular and controversial talk-radio shows broadcast out of this very building. Possibly using the same microphones and everything she was about to use. It was a little intimidating.

She settled on the couch and ran a hand over her hair. A snort escaped. She was going to be on the *radio;* it didn't matter what she looked like since only a few people would see her.

And one of those people would be Devin. It wasn't vanity or wanting to look good for *him* that sent her digging for lipstick. She was about to go talk to thousands— possibly hundreds of thousands—of people. She needed to feel confident. Even if they couldn't see her, the confidence of knowing she looked decent would come through in her voice.

It had nothing to do with Devin.

Hard on that thought, the door opened. Expecting it to be Kate, she finished with her lipstick and dropped it into her bag before turning.

Devin stood there, a slightly mocking look on his face. "It's radio, you know. No one can see you."

Do not take the bait. "It's a pleasure to see you again, as well." *Pleasure* might not be exactly the right word, since her stomach felt a little unsteady as he closed the door behind him, but at least her voice sounded normal enough to her ears.

Devin acknowledged the small slam against his manners with a mocking nod. He didn't seem happy she was here. Was he regretting inviting her on the show? Holding a grudge for her behavior the other day? He crossed to the fridge and took out two bottles of water. Handing one to her, he confirmed her earlier feeling. "I can't believe Kate convinced you to do this."

"Kate made some very valid points about controlling the press and putting the proper spin on things."

"Kate would sacrifice kittens on the air if she thought it would improve our ratings."

"So your plan is to sacrifice me?" A dread settled in her chest. Had she just walked into an even bigger disaster? Was this going to make things worse?

He shook his head. "This isn't *my* plan. Not by a long shot. I only learned of this bright idea as I was landing at O'Hare today. I've had to rearrange several things to accommodate you."

"Accommodate me? Kate said—" *Damn*. She should've... "Why didn't you return my call? We could have avoided this."

He shrugged. "The publicity was done. And I've been a bit busy today."

That remark reminded her how busy she *wasn't* at the moment, thanks to him and his stupid book. "I can imagine. A radio show, a book tour—it must be exhausting. How do you find the time to practice law?"

"I don't. Much."

"What?" That seemed impossible. Dev *loved* the law. Loved the tactics, the arguments, the logic required. Way back when, he'd spend hours explaining the nuances of a case or a statute to her, and his passion for law and justice had been one of the things she'd loved about him. She'd been floored to hear he'd ended up a high-priced and notorious divorce attorney, but to give it up altogether?

"My name may be on the door of the firm, but it doesn't mean I'm on every case. That's what partners and paralegals are for."

"Do you miss it?" The question was out before she could stop it.

"I don't have time for that either." She wanted to respond

to that, but Devin rushed ahead. "Sounds like you've done pretty well for yourself, *Dr.* Lowe. You became a psychiatrist after all."

"Clinical psychologist—" *no thanks to you* "—but you're close enough." As was she—just a few more months and she'd be official.

"And is it everything you hoped it would be?"

She could hear a small undercurrent in his voice that made her wonder if he was trying to pick a fight. No one else would notice it, but she knew that tone all too well for it not to send her hackles up. She lifted her chin. "And more."

"Good for you." He finished the bottle of water in one long drink and tossed it into the recycling bin.

Megan battled with herself. She'd sworn she wouldn't let her temper or her emotions control her and drive her to say or do anything that remotely resembled that debacle at the bookstore. She knew he was needling her. Intentionally. "Dr. Lowe" recognized that and knew how to handle it both properly and professionally. "Meggie," though, wanted to smack back.

Meggie won. "So how do you like being the country's divorce guru? Is it everything you hoped for while you were in law school?" She feigned confusion. "Oh, wait, that's not why you went to law school in the first place. Let me guess, there's more money in divorce than in protecting the Constitution."

"Lots more money." Dev had the audacity to grin at her and she felt childish for giving in to the urge to snark back. "Bit more excitement, too."

"And to think you used to be an idealist." The disappointment in her voice wasn't all fake.

"Blind idealism is dangerous."

"Ergo *Cover Your Assets?*"

"Exactly."

"And it doesn't bother you?"

"What?"

"The pessimism you dish out. Anyone listening to you would begin to believe that all marriages end in divorce."

He arched an eyebrow. "Wonder where I got that idea?"

She shouldn't have started this. They were already falling back into bad habits, and they hadn't even been around each other a full fifteen minutes yet. At this rate, they'd be at each other's throats by the time they went on the air. Time to be a professional—and the bigger person—and make a graceful retreat. "I tell you what—let's not make this personal." Dev's other eyebrow joined the first, and she quickly amended her statement. "Or more personal than it has to be, at least."

He nodded his agreement. "That's my plan."

"Good. I'm glad you have one. Why don't you fill me in on the details of this plan?"

"It's not too complicated, but if we're lucky it just might work out for you."

"And for you?"

That seemed to amuse him. "Megan, this actually has very little to do with me. I'm fine no matter what you say or do."

"In other words, you're doing me some kind of a favor?" She did *not* want to be indebted to him on top of everything else.

He just shrugged again.

"But you'll get a boost to your ratings, too."

"I'm number one in my time slot. My ratings don't really need a boost."

"But Kate said—"

"Kate's obsessed with our ratings. You know, maybe you could help her with that."

"If this works, and I get to go back to work, then I'll give her all the free counseling she needs." Biting her tongue to keep anything else from coming out, she faced him again. "So. The plan?"

"Simple, actually. First you'll need to bottle some of that hostility." Megan felt her jaw tighten. "Be friendly, but not too friendly. Polite. Noncommittal. Kate culled some of the more inflated speculations from the tabs and the blogs—we'll have a good laugh over that." That was an instruction, not a prediction, so she nodded. "The trick is to describe to the listeners how boring and mind-numbingly average our marriage really was and then make our divorce sound even more so. We'll take calls for a while, and then it will be over."

Over. She'd thought she and Dev were over long ago, but here they were. And to hear Dev describe their marriage as "boring" and "mind-numbing" felt like a slap across the face. Granted, they'd had problems—obviously—and that last year had gotten pretty ugly at times, but the early days had been far from boring or average. At least for her.

They'd been living on little more than love, but they'd been happy.

Dev obviously felt differently.

All her education and training had given her insight into why their marriage had failed, and she'd come to terms with that. She even knew what to say to couples going through the same things that split up her and Devin. She had perspective. She had distance. She had closure.

But hearing Dev dismiss their good times opened up all kinds of old wounds she didn't realize could hurt anymore.

Until right now.

Thankfully, Kate choose that minute to return, giving Megan a much-needed moment to get hold of herself while Kate and Devin discussed show-related things she didn't understand.

If she was smart, she'd back out of this crazy idea and go back to Plan A: lie low and ride it out. Plan B—changing her name and moving to Canada—was starting to gain traction, as well.

But then something beeped, and Kate and Devin were gathering up the few papers and bottles of water.

Kate turned her supermodel smile on Megan. "You ready? It's showtime."

Devin held the door open, waiting for her, and when she didn't move, that eyebrow arched up again. Irritation crawled over her, forcing her feet into motion.

She was walking to the gallows out of pure spite.

Dr. Lowe's official diagnosis? She was certifiably insane.

CHAPTER THREE

SHE'D MISSED THE FOURTH-grade field trip to the radio station, so Megan had spent last night trying to find out what she could about radio stations and how they worked. A couple of movies, so hopelessly out of date the disc jockeys were spinning vinyl records, some video clips posted on the internet...she still didn't have a clue. And she hated not having a clue. Research was her friend; it made her feel comfortable and confident. But the how-to's of radio were still a mystery, and she felt at a distinct disadvantage going into this.

That bothered her a lot. She didn't want to be at a disadvantage—of any kind—when it came to Devin. She needed to feel like an equal. She was, she reminded herself. She wasn't the same person she'd been all those years ago. She could hold her own—intellectually, professionally, sarcastically—against Devin Kenney.

She squared her shoulders as Devin opened a door marked Studio A. *I can do this.*

Two chairs facing each other across a small desk, two microphones, some computer screens—the booth looked a lot like what she'd expected from her research. Kate was on the other side of a large glass window that ran perpendicular to their table, settling into her chair and sliding large headphones over her ears. Somehow Megan knew Kate wasn't the kind of woman who would have "headphone hair" two hours from now. She, on the other hand…

Dev's "ahem" brought her back to the present. He was indicating a chair. "You'll sit here. That's your mic—be sure you get close to it, or folks won't be able to hear you. Here—" he handed her a set of headphones "—put these on. And don't touch anything."

Megan bristled. "I'm not five. I think I can handle that." Trying to look as if she did things like this all the time, she settled into the chair and smiled through the window at Kate.

"This is your last chance to back out, Megan. We're going to be live, and while there's a five-second delay, I won't be able to walk you through one of your panic attacks."

She almost let a sarcastic comment fly before she realized Dev had every right to be concerned about his show. It was the sign of a professional. She needed to respect that—at least while they were on the air. She'd keep her tongue behind her teeth if it killed her in the process.

She tried for a noncommittal tone. "I haven't had a panic attack in years, but thanks for your concern."

Dev looked surprised. "You haven't? That's a surprise."

"Do you think I could help other people if I couldn't learn to help myself first? I wouldn't have lasted long in this business if I couldn't talk to people."

"That's impressive, Meggie. Good for you."

She couldn't quite tell if that was grudging admiration in his tone or more sarcasm. She chose to accept the compliment, regardless of its sincerity. "Thank you. It means I should be able to get through this just fine." *At least I hope so.* She could feel all kinds of old insecurities bubbling up to the surface, and they felt much like a panic attack.

As Devin pulled his chair up to the desk, she realized how small the booth was. Not claustrophobic small, but not large enough to be in with your ex-husband sucking up all the oxygen, either. By the time she got her chair in place, only about a foot of space separated them. She tucked her feet under the chair, not wanting her legs and feet to accidentally tangle with his. *No footsie under the table tonight.*

Kate signaled them, and Devin put his headphones on. She did the same, and a panicky flutter started in her stomach. She took deep, calming breaths, trying to focus.

Through her headphones she heard Devin's theme music and intro. Then Devin leaned into the mic and started to speak.

It was as if his lips were only inches from her ear. She jumped, and her hands flew to her headphones, nearly pulling them off her ears in response to that baritone seeming to speak only to her.

She caught herself and pretended to adjust the headphones instead. Just another thing she hadn't prepared herself for. Her need to stammer seemed right on the end of her tongue, but Kate and Devin were bantering a bit, and the mention of her name returned her attention to the proper place.

"…welcome Dr. Megan Lowe, my ex-wife, to the show."

Both Devin and Kate looked at her, obviously expecting a response, and for a moment she faltered. Her heart thudded in her chest. How many people were listening? Every old insecurity she thought she'd buried was clawing its way to the surface.

Then Devin smirked at her.

A little spark of ire flared in her stomach, and that helped her gain control of herself. Trying to match his mock, she plastered a smile on her face, leaned into the microphone and prepared to meet the nation. "Thanks, Dev. I can't say I'm *pleased* to be here, but I appreciate the invitation, nonetheless."

He'd expected Megan to fold long before now. *Saying* she'd outgrown her shyness was a far cry from actually doing so, and he'd been ready to kill her mic and go to tape if she had a total meltdown. But twenty minutes into the show she sounded cool and poised, and her voice carried just a touch of mocking cynicism.

He'd seen the tiny flare of panic rise, but only someone who knew her very well would know that the wrinkle in her forehead was a warning sign of her discomfort. But the panic was gone as quickly as it had risen, and she managed to sound both amused and bored with the circus the media had made of her life and the outlandish speculation Kate had found on the blogs.

Megan's voice slid a notch down on the register as she leaned into the mic, giving her a seductive, husky tone that had to have half his male listeners at attention. He certainly was. When Kate commented on the main talking point— the fact Megan counseled couples to stay together when she herself was divorced—Megan chuckled.

She might as well have run a hand over him. The sound seemed to hum through his headphones directly through his body as if they were alone. Intimate.

He tried to shake off the feeling, but when Megan tilted her chin half an inch in his direction, he wondered if she'd done it on purpose.

No, Megan couldn't think she'd still have an effect on him after all these years. Hell, he wouldn't have dreamed it was possible if he hadn't felt the electric shiver over his skin.

Through the window Kate beamed an I-told-you-so grin,

but she would have been equally glad to have Megan crash and burn. Kate pointed at her computer, meaning the callers were lining up. A glance at his screen confirmed it.

Seemed as if Megan was on her way to fifteen minutes of fame instead of shame. He was oddly, *inexplicably* proud of her.

He brought the first caller on. "Caller, you're on the air."

"This is Andrea from Las Vegas. I'm a big fan of your show, Devin, but my question is actually for Dr. Megan."

Megan covered an amused snort with a small cough before she turned to him and mouthed, "Dr. Megan? Really?"

He shrugged.

Megan shook her head and leaned into the mic. "Hi, Andrea. What's your question?"

"So why'd you two get divorced? Who left who?"

Oh, he couldn't wait to hear her answer to this. When Megan looked to him, question written all over her pixie features, he folded his arms over his chest and shrugged.

Megan stuck out her tongue at him before she answered. "Devin and I were young when we got married—college sweethearts, in fact—and we had some maturity issues and some disagreements about what we wanted from our lives and each other. Those differences proved to be irreconcilable."

"So Devin left you?" It was more of a statement than a question. Maybe he should have warned her his listeners wouldn't accept vagueness.

He saw Megan's shoulders straighten. "Actually, I left Devin and filed for divorce."

At the caller's gasp of disbelief, he cut in, challenging Megan with a grin. "Hard to believe, huh?"

She rolled her eyes, but picked up the gauntlet. "Trust

me, Andrea, he totally deserved it." Her grin turned slightly evil, but her voice sounded conspiratorial. "He wasn't always this charming, you know."

"But surely he was still this hot, even back then. You had to be crazy to walk away from *that*," the caller continued, and through the booth's window he could see Kate practically crowing in glee as the queue of callers grew longer.

Megan cleared her throat. "There's a lot more to a good marriage than the hotness of one partner. Lust can only hold a couple together for so long—at some point there has to be something more. Some commonality. Some kind of meeting of the minds. I'm not implying that Dev's just a pretty face...." She trailed off, doing exactly that.

Kate was about to fall off her chair in excitement, and Megan shot him a look of triumph. The computer in front of him flashed as listener emails started flooding his in-box. It was time for him to take his show back in hand, damn it.

"Emotional stability helps a relationship, too. Both partners need to be mental adults." Megan's jaw dropped at the insult, and her eyes narrowed at him. He ignored her. "Thanks for your question, caller. Kate, who's next on the line?"

The next few callers were predictable—folks commenting on the hype and irony, asking them to confirm or deny more rumors—but as the show went on, there were a few callers who were, amazingly enough, more interested in getting out of their own marriages than how or why he ended his.

He was trying to explain—for the thousandth time—that covering one's assets did not mean hiding assets, since hiding assets was illegal in all states. The caller kept interrupting with bitter condemnations of his wife, as if that would allow him freedom with financial disclosure laws.

Pete-from-Tennessee harrumphed when Devin stopped to take a breath.

"Excuse me, can I butt in for a second?"

It was the first time Megan had commented on any question not directed at her or their past. He'd seen her shake her head a few times, and she'd probably bitten holes in her tongue, but she'd stayed off his "turf."

When he turned in her direction, he could see the frown between her eyebrows. She was drumming her fingers lightly on the desktop. "You have something to add, Dr. Megan?"

She frowned at his use of her new nickname, but she nodded to him before turning to the mic. "Pete, I'm hearing a lot of anger and a lot of bitterness. I'm not saying it's not justified, and without talking to you more or hearing your wife's side of the story, I can't offer any advice. *But,*" she stressed as both Devin and the caller tried to interrupt, "I'm also hearing hurt and jealousy, and that tells me there's something else going on. Have you talked about some of these issues with your wife? Or a counselor?"

"Megan..." Devin started, but she held up a hand to stay him.

"Well, Pete?"

Pete-from-Tennessee muttered something unintelligible. Then he cleared his throat. "Not everyone needs—or wants—therapy, Dr. Megan."

"I understand that. But something tells me you and your wife have some communication problems. You might benefit from a few sessions with a counselor."

"You're a shrink. That's how you make your money. Of course you don't think people should get divorced," Pete-from-Tennessee grumbled.

"On the contrary, I'd never advocate anyone stay in a marriage where they were mentally, emotionally, or physically in danger of any kind. There are some marriages that can't be saved." She met Devin's eyes evenly. "And there are some that shouldn't."

Then Megan's voice took on an earnest and almost hypnotic quality. The combination of compassion and concern tempered with a no-nonsense tone had even him listening carefully. "But from what you're saying, Pete, I'm not sure your marriage is firmly in either of those camps. Marriage isn't easy. Sometimes you have to fight for it. But it can be worth the battle."

They must have taught Megan that idea in graduate school, because that certainly wasn't her thinking when she walked out on *him*. The caller's sputters had lapsed into silence, so Devin asked the question hanging in the air. "You agree, though, that divorce is sometimes the best thing?"

Megan met his eyes again, and the mood in the booth shifted. "I do. Sometimes divorce is the best and the healthiest option for both partners. Some people just shouldn't be together. It's a cold, hard fact that can be difficult to admit, but once those couples split, they usually find themselves to be happier."

"What? No romantic notions about happily-ever-after or psychobabble—"

"Happily-ever-after isn't a romantic notion—but it's not guaranteed, either. Love and passion will only get you so far—like to the altar. It isn't always enough for a successful marriage."

Oh, he knew all about love and passion, and from the look on Megan's face, she was remembering a few choice moments from their history, too. But they also both knew the reality of it not being enough. He didn't break the stare, but he did try to inject a lighter tone to his next words for the sake of his audience. "Isn't *that* the truth."

Megan's brows drew together in a frown, and the intense stare changed to a dirty look. "Pete, do me a favor, okay? Talk to your wife before you get any more advice from a divorce lawyer. You may be partly right—I do tend to look for ways to heal a marriage. It's my nature and my job. But a divorce lawyer makes his money off your unhappiness and therefore has an unhealthy interest in your attempts to reconcile with your spouse."

Devin heard the caller take a deep breath. "I'll think about what you said, Dr. Megan."

Megan was good—he'd give her that—but the smug smile tugging at the corners of her mouth and the mocking lift of her eyebrows told him *she* knew it, too. He'd had a lot thrown at him in the past forty-eight hours, but this new side of Megan was the hardest of all to grasp.

"That's all I ask. Good luck, Pete, to both you *and* your wife. I hope you can figure out what's best for you both in the long term."

Kate took the opportunity to break in. "And on that note, we need to take a short break for your local news update and a message from our sponsors." A second later she indicated they were clear, and Kate began to gush. "You two are fabulous together! The chemistry is just amazing and the audience is eating it up. Have you seen the call queue? The mail piling up in the show's in-box? You guys are a hit! I knew you would be!" Kate wiggled in her chair, something he recognized as her "ratings dance." "Oh, and you have three minutes."

He took off his headphones and Megan did the same, a confused look on her face. "Three minutes of what?"

"A break." He moved the mics out of the way. "What the hell was that about?"

She'd started reaching for her water when he mentioned

a break, but his angry question had her responding in an equally snide tone. "What was what about?"

"Counseling my callers?"

"Sorry, but that's my job." Megan didn't sound the least bit sorry, and that tweaked his ire a little more.

"Not on my show, it's not. My callers want advice about breaking up, not psychobabble about making up."

"There was absolutely no psychobabble at all in anything I said to that caller. Just the truth. Maybe divorce is the best thing for that guy and his wife, but I'm not going to sit here and let you dish out all that bitterness on someone who might be able to be happy if you didn't egg him on and make him believe a divorce is the best idea ever."

"Sometimes it is. You said so yourself. And you would know, of course."

Megan's eye began to twitch. "You're not wrong about that. Trust me when I say that divorcing *you* was certainly the best idea *I* ever had."

I really do need some anger-management classes. Megan winced inwardly at the nasty remark that hung in the air between them.

Being around Devin—and the tension that proximity caused—was doing bad things to her brain and releasing the brake on her tongue. What had she expected? Things to be different?

Doing the same thing and expecting different results was the classic definition of insanity. *Doctor, heal thyself.*

But the words were out there now, and she couldn't see a graceful retreat from them. Too much of their past had been stirred up for that.

Dev's eyes narrowed, telling her she'd scored a direct hit with that outburst. "And yet you claim to be a marriage advocate. The hypocrisy doesn't bother you?"

Oh, now he'd crossed a line. "Hypocrisy? You're getting on your soapbox about hypocrisy? That's a laugh. You're the biggest hypocrite on the planet. And, again, I'm in a position to know *that* for a fact. Too bad it's not grounds for divorce in Illinois. I'd have gotten more alimony."

Kate's voice came over a small speaker. "Um, guys? I hate to interrupt—this looks, um, fascinating—but you've got one minute."

A muscle in Dev's jaw twitched. Oh, he was really itching for a fight now. But then, so was she. Going back on the air with him now might be a big mistake, considering how loose her tongue was today. But walking out now? In the middle of the show? That would only undo every bit of damage control she'd managed to accomplish tonight. There was no good to be found anywhere in this situation now. She was damned if she did, damned if she didn't.

Dev glared at her as he scooted his chair to the table and grabbed his headphones. "We'll finish this conversation later." He motioned her to silence as the red light came back on and Kate brought them back from commercial.

Megan had to give him credit—no one in Listener Land would know he was shooting daggers at her as she moved her chair and positioned her microphone. His voice carried none of the heat he'd just blasted her with as he started back into his show.

That lack sent warning shivers up her spine.

Kate motioned to her to put her headphones on. With a sigh, she did.

"Hi, caller, you're on the air."

"Hi, Devin. This is Terri from Albuquerque. I'm a long-time listener, but a first-time caller. And I just have to ask you and Dr. Megan something."

"Go ahead, Terri. Megan and I are open books tonight."

Dev raised an eyebrow at her in challenge. "No holds barred."

Megan shifted uncomfortably in her seat.

"What's the story with you two? You haven't really told us what the problem was."

Devin gave her a look that made her regret she'd let Kate talk her into this in the first place.

She was definitely moving to Canada.

CHAPTER FOUR

MEGAN KEPT UP A GOOD GAME for the listeners for the remainder of the show, but Devin could tell something was going on. She avoided eye contact unless absolutely necessary and when she did meet his eyes, she couldn't hold it for long. The technology in the booth seemed to fascinate her, but he could tell that interest was feigned. During the breaks she asked questions about how everything worked and even chatted with Kate some, but after that first heated exchange, all the fire seemed to drain out of her.

"Great show, guys." Kate cut the feed from the studio, ending their broadcast and turning it over to *Lola's Late Night Love Show* from a station in New York. "The mucky-mucks at corporate are going to be beyond thrilled. I got several calls from morning shows there toward the end."

Megan had been busily rooting in her bag, but her head jerked up sharply at Kate's words. "What do you mean, morning shows?"

"I mean you two were a hit and everyone is dying to know more. I'm going to be up all night cutting and redubbing to get the clips ready." Kate sighed dramatically, but the glee in her words couldn't be easily masked.

Megan, however, paled visibly at Kate's words. "This was supposed to be the end of it. 'Give them what they want so they'll go away,' remember?"

He laughed, causing Megan to finally meet his eyes directly. The anger and accusation there... "What gave you the idea the media would go away?"

"*She* did." Megan pointed at Kate, who shrugged and made a show of killing the mics and speakers, effectively bailing from the conversation by virtue of soundproof rooms.

He had no doubt Kate had led Megan to believe exactly that. "She lied."

Megan shot a killing look through the window at Kate, who was busy reviewing the tape and didn't see it. Then Megan rounded on him. "And *you* did, too."

"I never said anything like that."

"Yes, you did. 'We'll take calls for a while, and then it will be over.' Your words, in the lounge, not two and a half hours ago."

He thought back for a moment. "I was referring to the *show*."

"Oh, my God." Megan began to pace, her hands tugging at her hair, a sign of frustration he recognized from days past. "The morning shows...this is just going to make things *worse*."

Okay, this was an overreaction, even from Megan. "Media attention doesn't go away overnight, you know. This will take the nasty edge off, though, until it does."

Megan dropped into her chair with a groan and buried her face in her hands.

"That could happen sooner than you think, especially if something more interesting breaks."

"And what's more interesting than Devin Kenney?" she muttered into her hands. It wasn't a real question, so he didn't bother to respond. It wasn't his fault the book and the show were so popular, but Megan was acting as if he'd done all this to spite her somehow. Hard on that thought,

Megan lifted her head, spun the chair and faced him. "I hate you, Devin. I really, really do."

Actually hearing the words cut deeper than expected. "I'm supposed to be surprised? I figured that out a long time ago, Meggie. It's hardly news."

Megan's attitude changed. Her shoulders dropped, and while she was still obviously angry, somehow not all of it was directed at him anymore. "It's news to me. I didn't realize I was capable of that emotion until now."

"Really? If you walk out on people you *don't* hate, I'm curious to see what you do to the people you do."

Megan's jaw tightened. "I didn't just walk out on you. I *had* to leave because you were so caught up in yourself you forgot there was anyone else deserving of a thought from you."

"You're implying I somehow forgot we were married? That I mistook you for a roommate?"

"Pretty much." The sarcasm from Megan was new. Unexpected. It seemed graduate school had taught her a lot more than how to come out of her shell. It had given her teeth, as well.

"That's insane, Meggie."

"First of all, please do not call me Meggie," she snapped.

The heat behind what seemed like a simple statement caught him off guard.

She pushed to her feet to face him. "Secondly, I think I'm a bit more qualified to decide what's insane and what's not. And since I was there, since *I* was the one being treated like nothing more than a roommate, I know what I'm talking about."

Memories crashed in—vivid visuals of Megan's thighs straddling his hips, that long blond hair falling around them both like a curtain, her eyes closed and mouth open slightly in pleasure as she moved against him. A familiar, if almost forgotten, heat built under his skin. He fought to tamp it down. "I'm suddenly rather intrigued by your definition of *roommate*. Do you sleep with all your roommates, Megan?"

She gasped and her cheeks turned pink as she obviously got a similar visual. Then she swallowed hard and bit her bottom lip. Her arms crossed over her chest, pulling her thin cardigan closed, but not quickly enough to hide the sight of rigid nipples pressing against the cotton tank. The small success he'd had getting himself under control faltered.

"There's no need to be crude, Devin."

"It's a fair question. Personally, I'm not in the habit of having sex with my roommates, so I'm curious to see where you got *wife* and *roommate* confused."

Her chin went up. "A wife is normally afforded greater respect than a roommate," she lectured, ice dripping off her words. "Especially when it comes to big, important issues like where you're going to live, or what you're going to do with your future—your *joint* future. Your roommate can't expect you to take their plans into consideration when making yours. Your wife, however, should get a say. Since that seemed to be shocking news to you, I can only assume *you* were the one with vocabulary problems."

"And *I* think a wife would be happy her husband had been offered such a plum job after so many years of eating Ramen noodles and scrimping to pay the rent. I wasn't asking you to move to Cambodia, for God's sake. It's not like you couldn't have gone to school here in Chicago. And, hey, look where you ended up anyway."

"And you're still missing the point, Dev. I moved for you so you could go to law school—losing credits and pushing my graduation back—because you promised you'd do the same for me. But when the time came, I was supposed to walk away from *my* plans and dreams in favor of yours."

"And the obvious solution to a disagreement about jobs is, of course, divorce. I'm surprised you're allowed to counsel couples at all considering how quickly you found a divorce lawyer." The bitterness was back, surprising him with its intensity, but he had no reason to hide it now.

"Oh, grow up, Devin." Megan was good and mad now, and it was a completely different attitude and posture than he remembered. The pissy-pixie was gone, as was the big teary-eyed guilt-tripping he remembered. Somewhere along the line she'd found a steel backbone that had her in his face. "It was never just about your job or my school or anything else. It was the fact you were too freaking selfish to realize my plans should have any relevance in the discussion. I couldn't stay married to someone who could so blithely disregard me and my dreams.…"

"I'm the selfish one? Listen to yourself—everything coming out of your mouth is 'me, me, me.' That much hasn't changed about you. It's still all about you. Hell, this whole situation is practically a rerun. You don't like something, so you come to me and expect me to fix it."

"Son of a—" Megan bit the words off and took a deep breath. "Yes, I freely admit I was young and immature when we got married, and I probably did rely on you way too much. But I had to grow up pretty damn fast after I moved out."

"You moved out because you wanted to go to Albany and I wanted to go to Chicago. And instead of looking for a solution, you filed for divorce."

"Had you come to me and *asked* me to move to Chicago, I'd have done it in a heartbeat because I lov—" She caught herself and cleared her throat. "I would've moved to Chicago for you. Rearranged my life *again*. But you didn't ask. You just expected, and you went all sexist caveman when I didn't just roll over and do it."

"I thought your major was psychology, not revisionist history. How convenient for you."

Megan's eyes widened, and the flush coloring her cheeks and neck darkened. "Excuse me?"

"You've convinced yourself it was all my fault. I was the big fat jerk and you were the poor innocent victim."

Her jaw dropped and she quickly snapped it shut. "Stop. Just stop." The words barely escaped the hardened line of her lips. "I swear, Dev..."

Megan seemed to catch herself at that moment. Closing her eyes, she took a deep breath and let it out slowly. Then she did it again. When she opened her eyes and spoke, she seemed calmer. "Good Lord, I can't believe we're rehashing this. It's not beneficial to either of us. And it's certainly not healthy. We're way off topic." The angry crease in her forehead smoothed out and she sat.

The absurdity of the situation finally filtered through the adrenaline Megan caused to rush through his brain and body. "Agreed." They'd moved from spinning the media to spinning their wheels about the past. "If the APA or the Bar Association had witnessed that, they'd pull both our licenses."

Megan shook her head. "And the sad thing is that I know better." She leaned back in the chair and blew out her breath noisily. "There's now about four chapters of my dissertation I may want to revise before I publish."

"Megan," he began.

"Look, Dev—" she said at the same time. She interrupted herself and yielded the floor. "Sorry, go ahead."

"Ladies first."

She took another of those deep breaths. "You know, I do appreciate what you tried to do tonight. It's my fault I didn't quite understand what would happen. In retrospect, if I'd thought it all the way through, I'd have realized this wasn't quite the magic bullet I hoped it would be. But that's not your fault. Hopefully, it will help a little, maybe make it die down a little faster." She reached for her bag and settled the strap on her shoulder. "But now I'm going to go home and pack for Canada."

"That's a good idea. A vacation would do you some good. Maybe this will all be over when you get back." He doubted it, but Megan would be better off believing that. She could enjoy her vacation and be better prepared to face whatever was still being churned around in the press when she did get back.

Megan snorted and rubbed her hands over her face. She stood, then turned back to him, a question on her face. "I'm sorry. It's your turn now. What were you going to say?"

He thought for a moment. Megan seemed to be calming down, and spinning her up again wouldn't help anything. Neither would continuing their delightful trip down memory lane. The past was past, and as an adult, he should let it go and move on.

He'd show her who'd grown up and who hadn't. He would be the mature one if it killed him in the process.

"Do you need a ride home?"

Megan finally understood what drove some of her clients to drink. She'd always told them it was an excuse or a crutch, but at this moment she knew why so many people sought solace and calm in a bottle. She desperately needed a drink to calm her nerves, soothe her brain and numb a little of the unbelievably powerful and conflicting emotions tumbling through her.

But Devin… After everything that had happened tonight—including the amazingly painful opening of old scars—he seemed able to brush it all aside. Was Devin really that unfeeling now? Or did that coldness extend only to her? The idea bothered her a little at the same time she envied that ability. He'd gone from looking at her as if he'd gladly strangle her to calmly offering her a ride home without missing a beat.

"No, thank you. Kate sent a car...." She trailed off when Devin shook his head.

"Kate may have sent a car for you, but I promise she didn't arrange for one to take you home."

Every friendly feeling she'd had toward Kate had died off quite a while ago, and Megan was rapidly moving toward wanting to rip out Kate's beautiful shampoo-ad-quality hair now. She shot a dirty look through the window into the producer's booth, but Kate was busy with her computer. "I'll get the guard at the front desk to call me a cab, then."

"Don't be ridiculous. I drove myself in tonight, and I can run you home."

She wasn't about to admit to Devin that she didn't want a ride from him. She didn't want to put herself in another, even smaller enclosed space with him tonight. Although the tension built from their arguing and their past was making her desperately crave a glass of wine, she could handle that. She would be fine once she had a little time and distance to process the violent whirlpool of emotions in her stomach.

No, she didn't want to get into a car with Devin, because the one thing she couldn't process or even address right now—especially while he was in the same room with her—was the disturbing reaction of her body. Getting into the close confines of a car? Where it was dark and intimate? She had enough memories crashing in on her at the moment to deal with, and his flat-out remark about sex had made it impossible to ignore them. It was difficult enough to keep her mind away from their history, but to know that Dev was fully capable of—and probably *was* at that very second—picturing her naked and…and… She nearly lost it completely at that point.

And now she couldn't shake off the images of an equally naked Devin that were foremost in her mind and shaking up her libido.

"I appreciate the offer, but I'm sure it's out of your way.…"

"I don't mind. It's probably the least I can do."

Decision time. Continuing to argue with him over this would be juvenile, but there simply wasn't a graceful way to decline without sounding petty and petulant. Then there was the voice of her inner accountant who had calculated the fare for the trip home and was screaming to accept the ride if she wanted to make rent this month. Financial recklessness in order to make a stand? That was more than juvenile. It was stupid. And after the mess he'd put her in, he did at least owe her cab fare.

"Then I accept." She forced herself to smile as Devin opened the studio door and held it for her. Kate waved as they left, and it was all Megan could do not to make a rude gesture in return.

She really was losing her grip on her sanity.

Thankfully, Devin was quiet on the long elevator ride down to the garage under the building. He pulled out his phone and began checking messages, so she did the same. None worth responding to, but it kept her hands and eyes occupied and made being trapped in a small box with Devin a little easier.

The parking garage was all but deserted, and the hum of fluorescent lights bouncing off the gray concrete walls seemed like the setup for something in one of those bad horror movies Dev used to love to watch. It gave her the willies.

Devin must have noticed, because he called her on it.

She shrugged. "I just can't help but feel like that blonde girl in every horror movie right before the serial killer jumps out with a chain saw."

That caused Dev to laugh, and the sound had a disturbing effect on her stomach. "The blonde girl who dies is always alone. And usually wearing substantially less than you are."

The way Devin's eyes roamed over her as he spoke sent her mind back to earlier uncomfortable thoughts about states of nakedness. She tried to think of something witty to say, but her thoughts were a bit too scrambled. She settled for the nonwitty "Good point."

When she heard the beep of Devin unlocking his car, she finally took notice of the car he was headed toward. Low-slung, sleek and red, the car was every teenage boy's fantasy. As he opened the door for her, she let out a low, appreciative whistle. "Nice car. Divorce does pay well, it seems."

"That it does," he answered, then closed the door on any further comment she might have made. She didn't know much about cars, but even she could appreciate the butter-soft leather seats and dashboard that resembled a cockpit. When Devin slid into his seat and brought the engine to life, she could feel the horsepower rumbling under her feet.

Devin braced his hand on the back of her seat as he backed out of the space, and she got an unwelcome reminder of why this was such a bad idea. He was only inches away, and even the tiniest movement of his hand would cause his fingers to brush against the nape of her neck. Goose bumps rose on her skin and she fought back a shiver.

Of course Devin couldn't drive one of those huge SUVs, where a couple of feet would have separated them. Oh, no, the tiny sports car meant his arm brushed hers as he shifted gears, and every time she inhaled, the familiar scent of his aftershave tickled her nose. Once upon a time the scent had been comforting and calming. Not now. Tonight it jangled her nerves and made her palms sweat.

She had to get control of herself. "A red sports car is a cliché, don't you think?"

Devin shrugged. "I always wanted one. Don't you remember?"

She did, now that he mentioned it. A fancy car much like this one had always been Dev's wish when they played "One Day When We Are Rich." They'd drink off-brand beer and pretend it was champagne while they planned the fabulous vacations they'd take and the house in the country they'd buy.

It all seemed a little silly in retrospect, but it brought a small smile to her face before a feeling of sadness and loss for the kids they were and the dreams they'd had settled on her shoulders.

The feeling passed, though, when she realized Devin had achieved part of their dreams without her. "But now I know that sports cars are overcompensation devices for men who are, ahem, *lacking*."

Dev's smile was wicked in the half-light of the car, and she knew instantly she shouldn't have gone there. "I don't remember you complaining about my lack of anything. In fact, you seemed more than satisfied with my compensation."

Heat rushed to her face, and she could feel her ears burning. She refused to take the bait, though, and chose instead to move to the neutral topic of directions. Dev's eyebrow went up when she told him her address, but thankfully, he didn't press further.

They rode in silence for a few minutes, and Megan stared out the window at the familiar scenery to keep from trying to watch Devin's face out of the corner of her eye. It was ridiculous to be so uncomfortable. This was just Dev, for goodness' sake. At the same time, this was *Dev,* and that did funny things to her heart rate.

When he spoke, she jumped. "Everything else aside, you did well tonight. On the air, I mean."

She turned in time to see the side of his mouth curve upward at the last sentence. *Small talk. Excellent idea.* "Thanks. It was both easier and more nerve-racking than I thought. If that's possible."

"I understand. Not everyone does so well their first time."

"You're very good at what you do—on the air, at least," she qualified, and that got another smirk from Devin. "I can't say I agree with even half of what you said to your callers, but I'm impressed nonetheless."

Devin nodded at the compliment, and the question that had been on her tongue all night couldn't be held back any longer. "What happened to you, Dev?"

He looked surprised. "Happened how?"

"You used to have all this passion for justice and now you're a divorce attorney."

"Are you saying that there's no need for justice to be served in divorce proceedings?"

"Not at all. But I know you came to Chicago to do something bigger than argue alimony."

"Things work out differently than we plan sometimes." There was an undertone of bitterness to his words. She was familiar with the taste herself, so she couldn't blame him. "I was asked by my boss to help with a divorce for a client. It wasn't our usual thing, but we were doing it as a personal favor for that client. It was supposed to be simple and low-key. Instead it exploded, spinning completely out of control and hitting all the papers."

"That football player, right? I remember seeing your name tied up in that."

He nodded. "The longer it dragged on, the more salacious it got—mistresses and illegitimate children and accusations of abuse and extortion. And that's only what made the papers. The stuff that didn't would curl your hair. The division of property was a nightmare. I spent the better part of two years sorting out that one divorce." He snorted. "So much for simple and low-key. When the papers were finally signed and the dust settled, I had a line of folks with equally high-profile or messy divorces begging me to represent them."

She turned sideways in the seat to face him. "You're trying to tell me this was an *accident?*"

"Specializing in divorce, yes."

"And the show? The book?"

"Amazing opportunities I'd have been a fool to pass up."

Her perspective shifted uncomfortably with this new information. "So it's purely business, then. Not personal," she said partly to herself.

"What is?"

There was no good way to say this, but she was in too far now to back down. "There's that one blogger who insists your entire career was launched by *our* marriage and divorce."

That caused a laugh. "I had no idea you were so egotistical, Meggie."

Trust Dev to jump to the worst conclusion. "It would hardly be something I'd be proud of. I'd hate to think..."

"That you'd broken my heart and left me bitter and cynical?" Devin's sarcasm was back, but she couldn't deny it was appropriate.

"You can't deny you're bitter and cynical about *something*. I'm just glad to hear it's not me."

"If you'd witnessed what I'd witnessed in the last seven years, you'd be a cynic about marriage, as well."

Was he kidding? "You do remember what I do for a living, right? I've seen some of the worst marriages in the universe—and some of the worst people, I might add. I'm not all pessimistic and angry at the world."

"You always were an optimist."

"And you were an idealist."

"People change."

So neither one of them was quite who they used to be. "You're right about that."

"And you're certainly living proof of that." Dev shifted gears and his arm brushed hers. The hairs on the back of her neck stood at attention. Megan tried to unobtrusively move over and put a little more space between them.

"I'm not sure I'm following you."

"You've grown a pretty impressive backbone. And lost a lot of that shyness." There was admiration in his tone, but no trace of sarcasm this time.

"Like I said earlier, I had to in order to do my job. Getting out on my own and moving to Albany was a huge wake-up call. I had to find my spine. And my voice. I couldn't hide behind you anymore." She looked over in time to see Dev's jaw tighten slightly. "I don't mean that as any kind of insult to you. I was a different person then, and that wasn't your doing. It's just who we were. Who I was. But once we were over... In some ways, I owe you for who I am today. I'm sorry if you see that as some kind of insult."

The streetlights kept throwing Dev's face in and out of shadow, making it hard for her to read his face. Maybe that was a good thing.

"Well, Meggie, it's certainly worked out well for us both, then." His voice was as tight as her stomach.

The statement might be true, but the truth didn't lessen that feeling in her stomach. Thankfully, the conversation was about to end, and she grabbed the moment. "Turn left here, and I'll be the first on the right."

Devin expertly slid his flashy car into a space between two cars that added together probably wouldn't equal the value of one of his hubcaps. He shifted into Park and peered through the windows as she gathered her bag and unbuckled her seat belt.

"Thanks for the ride—"

His hand landed on her wrist. "*This* is where you live?"

She'd grown used to the shabby buildings, overgrown lawns and general dilapidation, but Devin's appalled tone brought back her own initial feeling about the neighborhood. "Yeah. Good n—"

The grip tightened. "I'm not sure it's safe for you to get out of the car."

She really wasn't in the mood for this. "Your car's in more danger than I am. So you should probably get it out of here before..."

Dev wasn't listening. "That building looks like it should be condemned. Tell me it's nicer inside."

She should, but the lie stalled on her tongue. "Where I live is none of your business."

"I'm not letting you out of this car, Megan, until I..."

God, she hated that tone. It brought back old, anger-inducing memories. As if to prove his point, Dev hit the button that locked her door. Irritation crawled over her skin. "What? You're going to kidnap me from my own front yard?"

"I'd probably be doing you a favor if I did. Jesus, Megan, why are you living like this? You have a job."

"I have an internship," she corrected, hating this entire conversation.

"And?"

She sighed. "You really didn't pay any attention at all to anything I ever said, did you?"

He didn't take the bait this time. Instead, his eyes bored into hers as he waited for an explanation. *I don't owe him one,* she reminded herself, but she found herself providing it anyway. "I have to do a two-year internship before I get my license. Internships are politically correct, modern forms of slavery—except that the slaver is doing me a favor by letting me work long hours for little or no pay. I'm lucky the Weiss Clinic pays enough for me to live *here.*"

"If you need money…"

"I'm paying my dues, the same as everyone else. In a couple more months I'll have my hours complete and I'll sit my exam. Then I'll be able to get a job that pays a living wage. Until then, I'm treating this as a character-building experience."

"So your newfound backbone actually came from living in poverty?"

"It's hardly squalor." She tried to sound upbeat. "In fact, it's not much worse than our first apartment."

He made an odd choking noise. "Our first apartment was a hellhole."

In retrospect, it had been exactly that. It just hadn't felt like it—unlike her current place. And she didn't need a

PhD in anything to tell her why her perception had been rose-colored back then.

Devin's grip on her arm tightened incrementally, bringing back those old feelings to tangle with the current ones. And that memory rush was simply too much to handle in the small, dark, cozy confines of Devin's car.

He was so close. Too close. She could feel the heat of his body warming the air around them, see the pulse in his neck. If she inhaled when he exhaled, they'd share the same breath. But she wasn't sure she could breathe.

And Dev seemed to realize that, too. His attention had moved from her neighborhood to her face and now seemed focused on her lips. Her heart skittered, skipping a couple of beats. Just another inch and she... *What the hell am I thinking?* She pulled back, putting as much distance between them as the car would allow, and Dev frowned.

She cleared her throat and chose her words carefully. "I appreciate your concern, but my life is not your business or your problem anymore. Good night, good luck and hopefully we'll never have to see each other again."

Feeling rather proud of her little speech, she reached for the door handle. Devin still held her wrist, and she stared at his hand pointedly until he released his grip.

The sounds and, unfortunately, smells of her neighborhood rushed in as she opened the door, destroying the quiet cocoon, and the intimacy evaporated. *Thank goodness.* "Bye, Dev."

"Damn it, Megan—" Dev began, but she closed the door on his words.

She climbed the stairs on unsteady legs, the imprint of his hand still burning into her arm. She didn't hear the engine start, so she assumed he was watching her make her way safely inside. That thought kept her head high. She just needed to get inside, get a drink and crawl under the covers to forget this hellish, hellish day.

The urge to look over her shoulder was almost impossible to resist, but she kept her eyes straight ahead as she opened the door. Leaning against it, eyes closed, she waited for the sound of Dev's engine revving and pulling away. It seemed to take forever.

As the rumble faded, Megan grabbed a bottle of wine from the fridge and headed to her bedroom. Then, for the first time ever, she changed the voice-mail message on her phone to have clients with emergencies call the clinic's answering service.

She couldn't deal with anyone else's problems or pain tonight.

She had enough of her own.

CHAPTER FIVE

MANNY'S AVARICIOUS GLEE was not what Devin wanted to face at ten o'clock in the morning. Not after the night he'd had.

Dealing with Megan and all the history they'd stirred up had left him with much to think about, and it had been nearly impossible to concentrate on anything else. After years of *not* thinking about her, having her that much on his mind was slightly disconcerting. When he'd finally given up and gone to bed, different memories awaited him. Making love to Megan in every position known to mankind for hours on end had left him grouchy this morning from lack of rest and the residual frustration of erotic dreams.

And now Manny had decided to show up first thing this morning, throwing off what little ability to concentrate he'd managed to find. To make matters worse, it seemed Manny had only one topic of conversation available to him today: Megan.

"My phone started ringing off the hook five minutes after you two hit the airwaves. The show was incredible. You guys were a hit."

"Kate would agree with you." Devin reached for the nearest file, not knowing or caring what it contained, and flipped it open purposefully. "Now, I've got a few…"

Manny was oblivious to the hint and got comfortable in

the chair next to Devin's desk. "Kate is a genius, a complete freakin' *genius,* for putting you two together. You know, with the offers I've heard this morning, you should seriously consider partnering with Megan for more projects."

That got his attention. "Have you lost your mind?"

"I'm serious as a heart attack. You should take your show on the road—do some rounds with the talk shows, some special appearances...."

"No thanks. I'm not interested, and I think it's safe to assume Megan isn't either." *But considering Megan's living situation, she could benefit from some paying stints....*

Manny didn't seem to hear him. "And The Powers That Be are giddy this morning. They want Megan to be a regular guest on the show."

He closed the file with a snap. "Absolutely not. Last night's freak show doesn't need to be repeated."

"Freak show or not, you and Megan together are magic."

Devin choked. Magic. *Yeah, right.* They'd had some magic years ago, but that was definitely gone. "Kate lied to Megan, and that's the only reason she was on the show to begin with. Megan would like this whole situation to die a quick death, and I can't say I object to that. For slightly different reasons, mind you."

"But—"

"No buts. This ends now. You work for me—not Kate, not The Powers That Be—and I want you to find something else to make money from. Something that doesn't involve Megan Lowe."

"I can't control the media. I'm good, but I'm not that good. Until something better comes along, you and Dr. Megan are what the world wants to see."

"Then *make* something better come along. Surely one of your other clients could be convinced to go into rehab.

Maybe one could pick a bar fight and get arrested? I'd be willing to make it worth their while." *Anything to end this.* "And yours, too."

Manny seemed to ponder his words, then shook his head. "Dream on, Devin. You're the media's darling right now."

He felt more like the media's bitch at the moment. And fortune's fool. A strong mental slap brought him back to earth. He couldn't get Megan off his mind because he'd never expected to cross paths with her again, much less twine his life with hers—however temporarily—and create a circus. The edge of frustration cutting him…well, that was just a side effect of the long, crazy hours he'd kept recently and the resultant celibacy caused by those long hours and ridiculous schedule. In a couple of weeks the hype around the book would die down, and life would return to normal.

Megan had just landed in his life at exactly the wrong moment, and that was the reason for his headache.

As Manny babbled on, he amended that statement. Megan wasn't solely to blame for his headache.

"Look, I have things to do today—other people's marriages to dissolve, people who are depending on me to end their misery. In order to do that, I need to file papers before close of business. You, the book and the show will have to wait your turn." He grabbed Manny by the biceps and hauled him to his feet. "In fact, I'm forbidding you to contact me—at all, in any way—until Monday. No email, no calls, no texts, no telegrams, not even a smoke signal from you until noon Monday. It will give you plenty of time to think of something else."

"But, Devin…"

"No buts. If I hear a peep out of you before twelve noon

Monday—not eleven fifty-nine, twelve—you're fired. Understand?"

Manny sputtered, but Devin was feeling pretty good as he guided Manny to his office door and out into the hallway.

"Devin—"

"This is the only warning you're going to get. Not a word from you."

They passed Kara, one of his paralegals, in the hall, and she dissolved into giggles as Devin frog-marched Manny to the reception area. "Kara, do me a favor and look up the termination clause in Mr. Field's contract." He tossed the words over his shoulder. "We might need it."

"Of course, Mr. Kenney. I'll get right on that."

In the tasteful, designed-to-impress reception area, he released Manny's biceps. "I'll talk to you Monday. Enjoy the long weekend."

Manny merely nodded, and Devin choked back a laugh. Manny's silence, however coerced, was both amusing and welcome. In fact, the prospect of an entire Manny-less weekend improved his mood considerably and he felt almost chipper as the door closed behind his overzealous agent.

His receptionist was openmouthed in shock when he turned around. She closed her mouth with a snap, but the smirk of satisfaction had him wondering how much his staff had resented Manny's constant intrusions on his office—and therefore everyone's time. A couple of his junior attorneys, several paralegals and a few secretaries—also wearing looks of amusement and satisfaction—lined the hallway as he made his way back to his office. "Now that we're less distracted, let's see if we can't get something accomplished today."

On that note, everyone disappeared into their offices and cubicles.

Blissful silence awaited him as he closed his office door behind him. He should've threatened to fire Manny months ago.

But as he started working his way through his in-box, an earlier thought kept pushing its way to the forefront of his concentration. Megan obviously needed money. Whatever her internship was paying, it was barely enough to keep a cat alive. Maybe she *could* benefit from this mess. Devin was sure Manny would know a way to make "Dr. Megan" some quick cash from appearances or something.

Without him, though. Megan and Devin were not a package deal. Not anymore.

If Megan was interested, he could drop Manny a quick email; it would smooth Manny's ruffled feathers to have something to wrangle into profitability over the weekend.

Oddly pleased, he whistled as he picked up the phone. This was a win-win situation. Any lingering guilt he felt over Megan would be appeased, and he'd make his agent happy, as well. Then he'd be able to catch up on things here and enjoy his weekend.

He loved having a plan.

"Are you *trying* to get fired? Is that your plan?"

Had she not heard Julie's ring tone, Megan would have continued to ignore her phone. The damn thing had been ringing nonstop all morning, disturbing her much-needed pity party. Dev had done a number on her head last night, and all the self-therapy in the world wasn't making it easier to cope. The last thing she needed was Julie's dramatics on top of everything else.

"What makes you think I have a plan for anything?" she

grumbled, debating whether she wanted to bother making coffee. Nah, the caffeine would only wake her up, and she had every intention of going back to sleep as soon as she could get Julie off the phone. If she could just sleep until this was over, that would be *grand*. "Anyway Dr. Weiss said I wasn't in danger of being fired."

"That was before. I think it's a distinct possibility now unless Dr. Weiss calms down."

"What?" That sent a jolt through her, chasing away every last bit of sluggishness in a way no amount of caffeine ever could. "Why?"

"You left here Monday with instructions to lie low. To let this blow over."

That feeling of dread she was beginning to think had taken up permanent residence in her stomach started to flow into her entire body. "Um, well…"

"What part of 'lie low' did you translate as 'go on the radio and stir up the whole country'? Dr. Weiss is having a duck this morning."

Dr. Weiss was emotionally incapable of having a duck. Or anything else. But if Julie seemed to think Dr. Weiss was remotely close… "Ah, damn it. Since when did she start listening to Dev's show? Did she hear it?"

"She has now. She missed the segment on *Chicago A.M.* this morning, thank goodness."

"Chicago A.M.?" Her voice came out as a squeak.

"Oh, yeah. It was a great piece." Julie's sarcasm cut to the quick. "Complete with a picture of you and a mention of the clinic."

Oh, no.

"The phone has done nothing but ring since eight this morning," Julie continued as Megan felt a chill settle into her blood. "The waiting room is buzzing because the clients are talking about it. It didn't take Dr. Weiss long to get the drift and then go online to get all the details."

The adrenaline of panic shot through her, making her hands shake slightly. "This is not good, Julie."

"That's an understatement. *Why* did you go on his show?"

She'd asked herself the same question a thousand times with no good answer. "Temporary insanity?" she offered weakly.

"Try that with people who don't know what that term actually means."

"I was trying to help.…"

"Megan, honey, get real. There's no help for this but time."

"I know that *now*. I just thought—I mean, I *hoped*…" She scrubbed a hand over her face and tried to regroup. "Should I call Dr. Weiss? Try to explain?"

"I wouldn't if I were you. She's a little unhappy with you at the moment." Julie fell silent and Megan prayed she was thinking of a brilliant idea. "Let me plead your case. Temporary insanity won't fly, but maybe I could argue for diminished capacity or something."

"Thanks."

"Don't thank me yet. I'm not sure Dr. Weiss is open to much discussion about you right now. We've heard your name a lot this morning, if you get my meaning."

Megan did. All too well. "Apologize to Alice for me, too. Let her know I'm sorry about all the phone calls she's having to take."

"Oddly, I think Alice is getting a weird thrill out of hanging up on them. It's not something she gets to do often." Megan could almost hear the smile in Julie's voice. At least there was something about this situation that didn't suck.

"Look," Julie added, "don't do anything else to rile Dr. Weiss. Stay home. Stay away from the media. And stay off Devin Kenney's show, for God's sake."

"Not a problem. I won't even call in to tomorrow morning's show. I promise." *Not that that would help.*

"Good. By the way, he's looking for you this morning."

She was still trying to force out of her head the image of her career going down the toilet. "Who is?"

"Devin. He called here and asked us to pass along a message to you."

Huh? "Why would he call there?"

"According to Alice, he knows you're not answering your phone this morning, so he called us figuring we'd talk to you at some point."

Lovely. "And the message?"

"He wants you to call him."

"Did he say why?"

"Does it matter? Didn't we *just* agree you were going to stay away from him?"

"I'm only curious," she argued, but she sounded weak.

She heard Julie sigh. "He didn't say why. Is that curiosity going to cause you to do something stupid now? Like call him?"

"Nope." Although she'd love to know what Dev was up to, she could resist. "Obviously it's not important or life threatening."

"Good girl. Keep that attitude and just stay home for the next few days. I'll try to calm Dr. Weiss down today—downplay what I can and put a positive spin on the rest. Maybe she'll calm down over the weekend and have a different attitude on Monday."

"I will. And *thanks*. I owe you."

"Oh, you definitely do. If I get fired for this, I'll never forgive you."

Megan flipped the phone closed, fully intending to get back to her wallowing, but instead she opened it again and scrolled through the call log. She had several voice-mail messages, but thankfully not everyone who'd called this morning had left a message. She scanned the numbers, wondering if one of them was Dev's. Would he have left her a message explaining why he was looking for her this morning?

It doesn't matter, remember? She had no need to talk to Devin about anything. Nothing good could come of it.

On that thought, she forced herself to get out of bed. Wallowing and moping weren't going to change anything, nor would they help, either. She knew that. She might have screwed up by going on Dev's show, but she could make the most of these unplanned days off and the forced seclusion. She'd revise and submit those journal articles, do some research she'd been putting off, maybe even paint her kitchen if she got really bored.

When this was over, she'd be able to go back to work with something positive to show—or maybe even impress—Dr. Weiss. All those projects she'd been putting off until she had time? Well, now she had it.

She went to her tiny kitchen to make coffee, and while it brewed, she made a mental to-do list. The pity party was over. By the time she had a full cup of caffeine ready, she'd shaken herself out of her funk.

Learn from this and grow from the experience. Think of possibilities. What doesn't kill me only makes me stronger. This was a learning experience, and though she'd stumbled coming out of the blocks, she could still finish well and salvage some of her pride.

And, hopefully, save her career, too.

* * *

Devin couldn't put into words why it bothered him that Megan hadn't returned his call. But it bothered him. A lot more than he liked to admit.

Surely she'd checked her voice mail or called in to her office. She had to know he wanted to talk to her. Of course, he could tell from speaking with the receptionist at her clinic that Megan was a hot topic today and that no one was happy about it, either. The woman had all but hung up on him.

Granted, they hadn't exactly parted as friends last night, but Megan wasn't the type to hold a grudge. Or she didn't used to be. Maybe she'd learned how to do that, too.

Regardless, he wanted to talk to her, and she wasn't returning his calls. This was business, and beneficial to her, so it was juvenile for her to ignore him when he was only trying to help.

And that was the *only* reason he was currently climbing the stairs to her apartment.

This place looked even worse in the daylight. While the neighborhood might have started off as working-class thirty or forty years ago, suburban flight and the ensuing income slide had taken its toll. *Seedy* was the nicest adjective he could muster.

And Megan lived here. She had a PhD, had graduated top of her class—if the press could be believed—and *this* was the best she could do. She'd left him to pursue her career and her dream, and she was living in a dump now. *This* was what she'd traded him in for. It was insulting. It boggled the mind.

The door rattled in its frame as he knocked. A moment later he could have sworn he heard a sigh before the rattle of multiple locks disengaging. Not that the locks would keep anyone out—a strong kick to the flimsy door would render them useless.

Finally the door opened and Megan leaned against it, annoyance written across her face. "What do you want, Dev?"

His comeback died on his tongue. Megan's hair was swept up and back into a messy coil, a pencil holding it in place. Her face was scrubbed clean, the sprinkling of freckles across her nose and cheeks dark against her fair skin. A pair of horn-rimmed glasses perched on the bridge of her nose.

He'd never harbored the sexy-librarian fantasy, but as the blood in his head rushed south, he could picture Megan taking off those glasses, pulling that pencil out and shaking her hair loose....

"Dev?"

The irritation in her voice snapped him out of his adolescent daydream and back to the present. The librarian fantasy stopped at her neck, as she was wearing cutoffs and a SUNY T-shirt, but the expanse of toned thigh revealed by those shorts awakened a new fantasy. After starring in last night's erotic dreamfest, Megan looked way too good for his loose grip on his sanity to handle.

He cleared his throat and tried to shake off the images haunting him. "I've been trying to get in touch with you."

"I realize that."

Her matter-of-fact admission she'd been intentionally ignoring him rankled. *"And?"*

She folded her arms across her chest. "And nothing. Can't you take a hint? I don't want to talk to you."

"But I want to talk to you."

Her eyebrows went up, reigniting that naughty-librarian vibe. "And that takes precedence over my desires because...? Oh, yeah, because you're Devin Kenney."

Desires. She should have chosen a different word. That

one was too dangerous to hear for someone still waiting for his blood to circulate freely again. Her desires, his desires...his body would like nothing more than to explore their *mutual* desires.

"I'm here to proposition you." Megan's jaw dropped, and he quickly caught himself. "I mean, I have a proposition for you. A business proposition."

"I'm not interested."

Was she *trying* to annoy him? "Don't be like that. You haven't even heard it yet. Aren't you at least curious?"

She sighed. Removing her glasses—but, sadly, *not* shaking out her hair—Megan pinched the bridge of her nose. "Fine," she conceded. "Come on in."

He was treated to an excellent view of her backside as Megan crossed the tiny living room and bent to lift a stack of books out of a chair. She added those books to a teetering pile on the floor and indicated he should sit. "Would you like something to drink? Water? Diet soda?"

He declined as he sat, and Megan took her seat on the sofa angling him. She curled her feet under her and leaned against the overstuffed arm.

The room, while bright with the afternoon sun, was depressing. The upholstery had once been floral, but it had faded long ago into an unrecognizable and threadbare gray. The apartment was clean, but decades of neglect showed in the cracked plaster and dingy linoleum. He recognized some of the artwork on the walls as being from their old apartment, but despite Megan's clear attempts to make the place homey or cheerful, nothing could overcome the sense of hopelessness that seemed to seep out of the walls.

Hell, the laptop on the opposite end of the couch probably cost more than the furniture in this room. He couldn't deny the small sense of schadenfreude that crept in. If she'd stayed married to him, she'd be living a much different lifestyle.

Megan picked up on his appraisal of her apartment. "Yes, I know it's a dump. But it's cheap, and it's clean and, most important, it's temporary."

"I didn't realize you were still an intern. When will you get your license?"

"I'll sit the exam in three or four months, depending on how long it takes me to get my hours finished, of course." She sighed and shook her head. "It will take a few weeks to get the official results, but I can start looking for a job immediately."

"That sure you'll pass, huh? That's kind of cocky of you."

She shrugged. "It's not cockiness. I'm damn good at what I do. You were pretty sure about the bar exam, remember?"

"Pure bravado."

"Liar." But she grinned as she said it, and it softened the pinched look around her eyes. "So what brings you by, Dev?"

Right. On to business. "You were quite the hit last night." At her smirk, he amended, "With the listeners and the corporate types, at least. Are you aware of your new popularity?"

"Oh, yeah." She didn't sound pleased about it.

"You obviously need some additional income." He gestured to the furniture. "And I could hook you up with the people who could turn that new popularity into a revenue stream for you."

"By...?" she prompted.

"By just being 'Dr. Megan.'"

She nodded her understanding. "I see. No, thank you."

God, she was frustrating. "You're jumping ahead again. You haven't even heard me out."

"I don't need to. I'm not going to be the equivalent of a newspaper agony aunt."

"It's lucrative."

"But it's not real. It's called psychotainment for a reason. You can't solve people's problems with a ten-minute sound bite." He started to counter that, but she held up a hand. "The people who call in to radio shows or go on TV don't really want help. They want a quick fix, and they usually get a pithy piece of psychobabble. Then they go back to their lives. Does it make a difference? There's no way to know. There's no follow-up. No aftercare. No actual solutions for these people. That's not me. It's not what I want to do with my life."

Megan could be so single-minded that the bigger picture often escaped her. "So you do a few appearances, make a name for yourself. That fame will build your real practice. I know that from experience."

She shook her head. "Most people who seek counseling—who *need* counseling—don't want anyone to know they are in counseling. Real clients would be afraid my notoriety would expose their weaknesses. They'd be afraid their problems would be fodder for my next appearance. I can't build a real career on a foundation that's all juicy show-and-tell."

"So you'd rather live like this?"

Her jaw tensed. "At least it's honest. And it will be worthwhile in the end. And at least I haven't sold out my principles." The defiant lift of her chin made that last sentence an accusation.

Anger pricked at him. "And you think I have?"

Megan clasped her hands together and leaned forward. Her voice dropped its edge and took on a smooth, impartial tone. "More important, Devin, do *you?* How do *you* feel about the choices you've made?"

Frustrated, he waved away her analysis attempt and leaned back in his chair. "Oh, don't try that with me. I'm not going to lie on your couch and tell you about my relationship with my mother."

"You don't have to. I know all about your mother already." She sat back with an exasperated sigh. "Unfortunately. Talk about someone who needed serious therapy." She shook her head. "I know she probably celebrated after our divorce became final, the grumpy old bat. How's she doing these days?"

The question caught him off guard, but there was no good way to soften the truth. "She died three years ago."

Megan's face fell, and she paled. "Oh, my God. I'm *so* sorry," she whispered. "I had no idea. What happened?"

"Heart attack. Seems she did have one after all."

"Dev," Megan chided.

This was yet another reason not to hang out with his ex. She knew way too much. "Don't worry, Dr. Megan, I'm good."

"You aren't talking to Dr. Megan. You're talking to me, and while I probably know more than you're comfortable with, I'm still willing to listen."

He regretted snapping at her. Megan's sympathy seemed genuine. "Mom and I made our peace before it happened." A flash of surprise crossed her face before she nodded. "So there's no need for me to go into therapy."

"I'm glad to hear that. Really I am." Considering how his mother had treated Megan, he was surprised at her sincerity. "What about your dad?" she continued. "And your sister?"

"Both fine. Dad moved to Arizona to be closer to Janice and her kids."

Megan's eyes widened. "Janice has kids?"

"Three boys." This conversation now bordered on

surreal—the how's-the-family catch-up—but it felt rather nice at the same time.

"Wow. Tell her I said hi the next time you talk to her."

"Will do. I think she missed you after the divorce."

"I missed her, too."

Anyone else? Did you miss me? Did you miss us? The questions popped into his head, but he pushed them aside. It was his turn for the small-talk questions. "And your folks?"

"Both fine. Hale and hearty. Mom's trying to talk Dad into moving to Florida when they retire."

Roger Lowe was too set in his ways. "Your dad's not going to move south."

"I know that and you know that." She smirked. "I think Mom knows that, too, but she's not willing to give up the fight just yet."

"Good for her."

Megan laughed—a real laugh this time—and adjusted her position, relaxing against the cushions, stretching her legs out and propping her feet on the coffee table. The table wobbled ominously, on the verge of collapsing on itself.

That brought him back to the purpose of his visit. He wasn't here to wander down memory lane or catch up on each other's families. "About that offer…"

Megan tensed a little, and the conversation lost its easy tone. "Again, thanks, but no thanks. I know a lot of people would welcome the chance in the spotlight, but surely you realize I'm not one of them. I'm not comfortable being 'out there.'"

"You fooled me. You seemed like a natural. No one would ever be able to tell you used to hate any kind of public speaking."

"I appreciate the vote of confidence, but just because I'm not that painfully shy mouse anymore, that doesn't mean

I'm ready—or willing—to let it all hang out. But it means a lot to me that you think I even could."

Megan's hand landed on his and squeezed. She probably meant it to be a friendly, meaningless gesture, but the contact rocketed through him. The first deliberate touch in over seven years, and it set his skin on fire in a flash.

Megan jumped, and when her eyes flew up to meet his, he knew she felt it, too. Belatedly, she tried to move her hand away, but he caught it easily.

A slow flush rose out of the neckline of her shirt, creeping its way up her neck until her cheeks turned red. Her thumb moved slightly against his skin, a faint caress he doubted she even realized, but it fanned the flames licking his skin. He returned the movement, his thumb teasing lightly over the skin of her palm, and her breath caught.

The silence stretched out, neither of them moving except for the gentle stroke of their fingers. It was ridiculous, this connection and the sensations it caused, but he couldn't bring himself to break the contact. Megan seemed to have a similar problem as her pupils dilated and her teeth worried her bottom lip.

It would be easy, so easy to... One tug, and she'd be in his lap....

"D-Dev...I...um...I..." she whispered, and he felt her tremble ever so slightly. Megan closed her eyes as her tongue moistened her lips. She shifted her body forward as he reached for her.

The coffee table collapsed from the increased weight, sending books and papers crashing to the ground. With the table supporting her feet gone, Megan overbalanced and landed on the floor with a thud and a colorful curse.

Her hand was still in his, and he pulled, helping her right herself. "Are you okay?"

Big blue eyes met his and he watched as several emotions

battled for dominance. The desire was still there, but banked, while amusement and embarrassment and annoyance seemed to be gaining ground.

She pulled her hand away and used it to push back the hair that had escaped its containment when she fell. "I swear, Dev, being around you is a disaster looking for a place to happen."

CHAPTER SIX

MEGAN HAD MEANT THE WORDS to be light considering the embarrassing position she was in—and the even *more* embarrassing position she'd just escaped—but somehow they seemed to come out all wrong.

She'd known the moment she'd seen him on her step that nothing good could—or would—come from letting him in. She'd spent the day convincing herself of that and focusing on the future instead of the past. But she could no more close the door in his face than sprout wings and fly.

Dev just had some kind of unholy control over her. She thought she'd broken it when they split up, but if anything, the past couple of days had proven *that* notion false. Hell, the past five minutes had proven it to be a bald-faced lie.

And now Dev was in her tiny living room, filling the space and leaving her light-headed and shaky. Even worse, the heat in his stare didn't abate as she untangled herself from the mess on the floor and the remains of her coffee table.

She picked up a table leg and examined it, eager for something to distract Devin while she got her own hormones under control. "The apartment came furnished. I wonder how much they're going to charge me to replace this."

"I'll pay for it." The growl in his voice sent shivers over her skin and kicked her pulse into high gear. "Megan—"

"That's okay." She cut him off before that growl could go somewhere else, and hated herself for taking the cowardly way out. What happened to standing up to him? "I'm sure any local garage sale will have a replacement for a couple of dollars." She laughed weakly, but Devin didn't join her. He was still staring at her, his eyes raking over her body and leaving heated skin in their wake. Dev might have shown up at her door with a business proposition, but she knew that look well enough to know he had something entirely different on his mind now.

So did her body. It was completely on board with the idea, conveniently forgetting that they weren't a couple anymore. She could feel the early trembles of arousal in her thighs, the sensation traveling up to make her core muscles clench in anticipation.

Even worse, she knew Devin knew it, too. Electricity snapped through the air between them, the tension growing thick and heavy. She had to do something to break the spell or else...

"Meggie..."

That husky tone nearly did her in, pouring gasoline on the fire he'd started with just a look. *No,* she told her libido. *This is not going to happen.* She had enough problems without compounding them by getting naked with Devin.

She levered herself to her feet, only to find her knees weren't steady enough to support her. As she wobbled, seeking her balance, Devin's hand closed around her wrist, pulling her gently yet purposefully toward him.

Be strong. What had happened to the anger, the outrage, the indignation that had kept a nice safe wall between them? It had crumbled under one passionate look. *So much for being over him.*

It took every bit of strength she had to override her hormones, pull her wrist out of Devin's grasp and dig her heels into the floor. "Dev," she started, but her voice sounded thick. She cleared her throat and tried again. "Devin, I, um…I appreciate your offer."

His eyebrows went up and she hurried to clarify. "The offer to help. Business, I mean. You've done all you can and you were right last night when you said it would just take time. I think I'll go back to that plan and wait this out."

With the moment of connection broken, the heat started to fade from Devin's eyes. Then, with a quick shake of his head, it was gone entirely. Envious, Megan wished she could do the same, but at the same time she felt a little hurt he could turn it off so quickly. She, on the other hand, still wasn't steady on her feet and parts of her were throbbing along with her rapid heartbeat.

He cleared his throat. "That's probably a wise choice."

Damn it. "Yeah." She squatted and began sliding the papers and books into slightly more orderly piles. It gave her something to do with her hands, something to look at other than him, while she shored up her already faltering resolve. "So…I'm going to get back to work. I've got a ton of research to go through.…"

"So I'll let you get back to it." He stood, looming over her position on her knees on the floor.

She quickly scrambled to her feet. "Thanks."

"If you change your mind…"

I'm about to, if you don't leave. "I won't," she answered quickly, clutching a psychiatric manual to her chest like a shield.

His lips twitched slightly. "I meant about exploring some of those other media options."

Kill me now. Her ears burned with embarrassment. "I'll keep it in mind and let you know. Okay?"

"Okay. Bye, Megan."

"Bye, Dev." She closed the door behind him and threw all the locks. Only then did she release the breath she was holding.

She made her way to the bedroom on unsteady legs and fell face-first across the bed. Disgust at herself churned the acid in her stomach. Embarrassment and humiliation had her skin crawling. But under that, she *burned.*

For Devin.

She was not some teenager without control over her hormones. She was an adult, damn it.

An adult who knew exactly what Dev could do to her.

Exactly, she told herself as she pulled a pillow over her head. Physically, yes, Dev could do amazing things. Things that made her shiver at the thought. Her body was screaming at her to call him back and take him up on the unspoken yet blatantly obvious offer. She could practically feel his hands sliding over her skin, and gooseflesh rose in anticipation. Devin was generous, thorough, often insatiable.... Ah, yes, *physically,* there was no downside.

But she also knew what Dev could do to her emotionally. And her reaction to him proved beyond a doubt that her emotional state wasn't as stable as she'd thought. The tug on her heart couldn't be ignored and it scared the hell out of her. The magnetic pull she'd felt had been more than physical, more than just a chemical reaction or memories of how good it could—would—be. *That* was something else entirely.

Her whole life was in too much upheaval to add *that* to the mix.

Deep breaths and rational pep talks weren't helping. She focused on the only thing that might—the anger and hurt that had driven them apart last time. When she had no luck with that, she flipped to her back and concentrated on the present—her problems that wouldn't be helped by giving in to the chemistry between them.

That was no use either. With a sigh of disgust, she pushed herself off the bed and headed for the bathroom.

She'd try that old standby, the cold shower.

Learn from your mistakes. Devin couldn't count the number of times he'd lectured his listeners on that very topic. For that reason alone, he had no excuse for what had almost happened. If Megan hadn't chickened out and all but thrown him out of her apartment, it wouldn't have been *almost*.

And while he could beat himself up over the fact he should know better, he also knew he wouldn't have regretted it for a second. Whatever lie he'd told himself on his way to Megan's, the real reason he'd gone to her had become crystal clear the moment she touched him.

Getting involved with Megan—in any way, for any reason—was just plain stupid, but that knowledge wasn't damping his raging erection or blurring the erotic images in his mind. Between the two, he was getting nothing done tonight.

Something had to give, or he was going to lose his mind.

Sure, he felt sorry for her, for the situation she was in. Her notoriety was partly his fault; even if he hadn't directly caused it, he'd compounded it, and any decent human being would want to help.

But this other need… That had nothing to do with being a decent human being. In fact, a decent human being wouldn't compound a bad situation by acting on what he was feeling at the moment.

It wasn't going to stop him, though. He'd just have to accept he wasn't a decent human being. He'd been called worse. By Megan, in fact.

But Megan's reaction proved this wasn't one-sided. She wanted him—that much had been very clear—but she was fighting it. Probably for all the same reasons he'd examined and rejected already.

Devin scrolled through the messages in his in-box again. There were many things he should be working on, but none really captured his interest.

He could be at Megan's exploring his new naughty-librarian fantasy. Or multiple other fantasies. Other people's soon-to-be ex-wives weren't nearly as interesting as his, so he clicked the email window closed and gave up the pretense.

This was sick. This was twisted. It was nuts to even consider.

But it was going to happen. That much he was sure of. And he was pretty damn sure Megan felt the same way.

Maybe if they could both get it out of their systems, then they could go back to their separate lives.

Now to get Megan to see it that way.

"I'm fine, Mom. Really." The lie got easier each time Megan told it. Another three hundred times and maybe she'd begin to believe it, as well.

"Well, if it makes you feel any better, I think you did great on Devin's show. I'd sign on as a client of yours any day." Her mom was in cheerleader mode—had been since the first whiff of trouble.

"Thanks, Mom. But please tell me you and Daddy aren't having problems."

"Nothing a move to Florida won't solve."

"Together, I hope."

"Of course, honey. Don't worry about us. We've been married so long divorce isn't an option. I might kill him, but I won't divorce him."

"Good. But try not to kill him, either. Call me first and I'll talk you down."

"Speaking of killing people…" Her mom's voice took on a too-casual tone and Megan braced herself. "How are you getting along with Devin?"

Argh. "What do you mean?"

Mom sighed. "You've obviously had to spend some time with him—during the show, if nothing else. How'd that go?"

"Fine," she managed to get out in a normal tone. Thank goodness her mother couldn't see her face. She'd be busted for that lie for sure. "We've both grown and changed and we're different people now, and this was a professional setting and situation, so it—" Megan broke off midramble as her mother laughed. "Okay," she admitted, "so I've had better moments. You just said it all sounded fine on the radio, and that's what matters."

"If you say so."

"I do." *I need to change the subject.* "So, Mom—"

"Did you listen to his show this morning?"

She had, but she wasn't going to admit it. "Are you telling me you did?"

"Of course. I wanted to see which way the wind was blowing. Make sure he didn't undo any of the progress you'd made. He didn't, by the way."

"I didn't think he would." But she'd listened to be sure. "Devin's being great about this. He understands my predicament."

"So did you two talk about anything…?"

Not subtle, Mom. Not subtle at all. "Oh, Mom, there's someone at the door. Can I call you later?"

"Of course, honey. Take care."

Megan hung up and spent a brief moment feeling bad about lying to her mother. After all the Devin-related drama of the past, though, of course Mom was twitchy about her being anywhere near him again.

And boy, did Mom have good reason to be. Megan was very twitchy about it, too, but after a long, sleepless night spent thinking, she had it under control now. The current emotional upheaval made her vulnerable. That vulnerability had her looking for a safe anchor. Years ago that anchor had been Devin, and with him here now, she was misplacing all that angst and emotion and need. That was the explanation for yesterday's close-call chemical reaction.

Now that she'd identified it, she could avoid it. She felt much better today with her newfound understanding of the situation. Sadly, that understanding hadn't completely squelched the ache inside her, but it had damped it down a bit. Once she managed to rein in her subconscious's need to explore every old fantasy she'd ever harbored, she'd be in good shape. It would just take a little time. And effort.

Maybe in a couple of days—or months—she'd be able to articulate that to her mother. Until then, avoiding discussing the issue seemed wise.

She left the phone on the couch, stepped over her laptop and headed for the kitchen for a refill. As she opened the fridge, she heard a knock at the door.

Spooky. Either she'd gained ESP recently or something was telling her not to lie to her mother about things unless she wanted them to come true.

At the door, she looked through the peephole and nearly fell back in shock.

Devin. Here. Again.

Why?

She weighed her options. Honestly, she had only two—open

the door or pretend not to be home. After yesterday... She took a careful step backward.

"Megan, I know you're home." Dev's voice carried easily through the flimsy door. "I can hear you moving around."

Damn it.

"C'mon. Open up."

She took a deep breath to steady herself. Blowing it out slowly, she opened the door.

Dev grinned at her. "Hi."

"Hi, Dev, what's..." She trailed off as she saw what he was holding. "What's that?"

"What does it look like? It's a coffee table."

Like that's normal? "Well, yes, I see that. But...but... *why* do you have a coffee table?"

"To replace the one you broke yesterday."

Her head was spinning. "That's not neces—"

"This is where you say, 'Thanks, Dev,' and invite me in. It's heavier than it looks."

She stood there gaping as Devin turned sideways to pass her and stepped inside. He carried the table to the center of the room and set it down carefully. "There. It doesn't match the sofa, but then nothing in here does."

I've snapped. The stress has gotten to me and this is a hallucination. She closed her eyes, and when she opened them, Devin was still standing in her living room. With a coffee table. *Okay. Reality is just weird.* Closing the door, she tried again to make sense of the situation. "It's lovely, Devin, and that's very kind of you, but..."

"You're welcome." Devin looked at the mess covering her floor. "You certainly need it. How are the articles going?"

Confusion reigned supreme. "Devin...um...I mean,

what…" She scrubbed a hand across her face. "What is going on?"

Devin frowned at her, obviously assessing her sanity and getting a big question mark. "This—" he indicated the table "—is a gift. For you. Why are you looking at me like that?"

"Because you showed up on my front step with a coffee table for some unknown reason. I think I'm allowed to be a little thrown by this."

That got her a shrug in response. "I don't see why."

She held on to her last shred of sanity. "Devin…"

"Okay, so I'm feeling a little bad about the stress you're under, so I thought I'd try to do something nice for you."

"So you bought me a *table?*"

Devin's smile bordered on sheepish, but she wasn't buying it for a second. "It seemed like a better idea than flowers or something. I knew you needed a table."

A laugh bubbled up without warning. It felt good after all the tension of the past few days. "You're certainly full of surprises, Dev."

He looked pleased with himself. "I try. Now, are you going to invite me to sit and stay awhile?"

She shouldn't. She knew that much for sure. But he'd brought her furniture; she couldn't just send him off like a delivery guy with a smile and a wave. With all her new-found answers gleaned from her self-therapy last night, surely she could handle a polite conversation with the man. After all, he was trying to be nice. "Would you like to sit? Can I get you something to drink?" When he shook his head, she went to the couch and sat, trying to shake off the déjà vu with simple, harmless small talk. It proved harder than expected, though, as she fumbled for a topic. "I listened to your show today. It's a bit different than the nighttime version."

He seemed shocked at her revelation, but then he shrugged. "Different target demographic. There's some overlap, of course." With a level stare, he added, "And you still don't approve."

"I don't have to approve. Or agree with what you're saying. I may think you're wrong, but it's your show. Your listeners." She shrugged.

"And you'd tell them something different?"

"Not necessarily. I mean, if people are definitely getting a divorce, then they really do need good advice on the legal aspects. It's the folks calling you who seem on the fence that I worry about."

"And yet you look down on psychotainment. For some folks, that sound bite is the best they're going to get."

He had a point. "True," she conceded, "but I don't have to like it. On the other hand, it's not my show, and it's a free country. You're obviously popular, so I'm in the minority. I'm okay with that, and I'll keep my objections to myself." To prove it she folded her hands in her lap and smiled.

Dev's eyes widened in surprise, and she was treated to one of those dangerous grins. "Boy, if I get this just from bringing a coffee table, what will I get if I show up with a couch?"

"Do *not* show up at my front door with a couch, Devin Kenney. Or any other furniture, for that matter."

"So it's the furniture you object to, not the delivery guy?" Dev winked at her.

Busted. "Well, um…I wasn't really expecting you at all. Much less with a table." *Nice recovery.*

Dev simply laughed.

Time to get this back in hand. "Okay, I know why I'm home on a Friday afternoon, but don't you have a job you need to be at?"

To her utter amazement, Dev leaned back in the chair

and got comfortable, propping his feet on the new table, which on second glance looked very expensive. "Yes, but I also have plenty of people to take care of the grunt work. They'll call if they need me. I thought you might need the company, though. You seem determined to be a recluse."

The sight of him settling in unnerved her. "Staying in is often good for people. Gives you time to think. Accomplish things. Do stuff." *Stop babbling.* "Things you normally wouldn't do."

"So I can talk you into having dinner with me, then."

"No!" She caught herself and tried again. "I mean, thanks, but no."

"Why not? That's not something you'd normally do."

Because I'm not that crazy. Lord, she had to get control of this situation. Fast. "Is there a particular reason you're here, Dev? Other than furniture delivery?"

She regretted the question immediately. A dangerous spark lit in Devin's eyes as they met hers, and that was all the answer she needed. She should feel insulted, irritated, maybe even outraged, but her traitorous body was too primed not to react to the electric current flowing between them.

That electricity sent a jolt through her that had her jumping to her feet. "Damn it, Dev."

The slow, sensual smile she got in return caused her knees to wobble. *Oh, no. No, no, no.* So much for all those answers and explanations and reasons she'd worked out so carefully. They toppled like dominoes after one look from him. It was ridiculous, frustrating....

"Come here, Meggie." He softened the command by wrapping his hand around her fist, causing her fingers to release so they could twine through his. Palm to palm, the connection was complete. Electric. It hummed through her, bringing dormant cells back to life and making them pulse with need.

He lowered his feet to the floor and tugged her arm, bringing her a step closer. To him. Into the energy that radiated off him like a sexual aura.

Yesterday she'd been strong. Dug in her heels and stood her ground. Until this moment she wouldn't admit—not even to herself—that she regretted that stance.

She could make a different choice today.

The part of her brain that could quote the textbook on why it was a really, *really* bad idea to even consider what she was considering launched a protest, but her body wasn't listening.

One more tiny step and she was standing between his thighs. Dev's head was at eye level with her cleavage, and her nipples hardened in anticipation. He released his grip on her wrist, only to slide both hands up the backs of her thighs, causing her to lean ever more slightly toward him and the promise in his eyes. His thumbs brushed under the hem of her shorts, teasing the sensitive skin at the curve of her bottom.

"Dev—" Her voice was a broken whisper, so she cleared her throat to try again. "Dev, I'm not sure this is a good idea."

"It's a *great* idea." His voice was husky with need, hypnotizing her. "We've been heading here since you crashed my book signing on Monday. I know you, Meggie. And I know you want me as badly as I want you right now."

CHAPTER SEVEN

DEVIN'S BALD WORDS affected her as strongly as the fingers caressing her inner thighs. *Walk away, Meggie, walk away.* But the message wasn't reaching her legs. They wobbled again, and she had to place a hand on Devin's shoulder for support. The heat of his skin burned her, even through his shirt, but she couldn't let go. "This isn't about want." She wasn't sure which of them she was trying to convince.

Devin called her bluff simply by placing his lips at the hollow of her throat, letting his tongue sneak out to feel the frantic beat of her pulse. Her breath seemed trapped in her lungs.

His hands slid up to her waist as he lifted his head. "You're right," he said, and disappointment caused her stomach to clench painfully. "It's about need."

That was all the warning she got before he pulled her head down and captured her protest in his mouth.

With one touch of his tongue, everything she'd told herself since the day she left was proven a lie.

She recognized his taste and the weight of his lips. Like magic, she slipped back into the rhythm she thought she'd forgotten long ago, matching the movement of his kiss. The hand on his shoulder slid up along the tight cords of his neck, finding the soft, fine hairs at his nape.

His hands cupped her jaw, holding her head steady, but

there was tenderness under the pressure that caused her heart to skip a beat. When Devin released her face, letting one hand tangle in her hair while the other slid slowly to the hem of her shirt, the poignancy of the loss was quickly replaced by the flash of heat from his bare hand against the small of her back.

Her body seemed to remember and respond without reservation, eager to receive his touch and the pleasure it knew would follow. As Devin tugged her shirt up, her arms floated up without hesitation, offering him access. Once the fabric cleared her head, Dev's eyes were on hers as he swept his hands down her ribs and up to cup her breasts through the thin cotton of the simple bra she wore. Every stock phrase she'd perfected with her clients came screaming into her head.

This is all misplaced—emotions dragged out of the depths of her psyche due to the happenings of the past couple of days. Digging through the past had awakened all kinds of memories, and this was simply a side effect.

She felt the clasp of her bra give way. *This isn't real.*

Devin's tongue traced her collarbone as he slid the straps down her arms and off. *This is a really bad idea.*

She arched as Devin's thumb scraped across her nipple, and his mouth found the sensitive place just below her earlobe. *You'll regret this later.*

Her hands pulled at Devin's shirt, working it up and off, and exposing the hard planes of his chest for her to trace with her fingers. *It won't solve anything. In fact, it will only complicate the issue and make things worse.*

Then Devin's hot mouth was on her breast, closing around an aching nipple and tracing it with his tongue.

And she no longer cared about the possible repercussions.

She gripped Devin's shoulders for support and gave herself over to the moment.

Devin knew the moment Megan quit arguing with herself and gave in, and the knowledge electrified his skin. *This.* Seeing Megan again, having her haunt his dreams—even rehashing their past—it had all been leading to this. To having Megan's skin under his hands and pressed against him again. Having her scent on him, her taste in his mouth. The intoxicating combination made him light-headed as he moved to tease her other breast, then burned him as the old flame kindled a raging inferno.

He pushed to his feet, wrapping Megan's legs around his waist and holding her hips as he headed for her bedroom. She groaned softly as she tightened her legs and moved restlessly, nearly causing his knees to buckle as pleasure shot through him.

Megan's bed was a tangle of covers, the pillows tossed haphazardly against the headboard, her quilt sliding half-way off the edge to the floor. Some things didn't change, it seemed, but Megan's unwillingness to ever make the bed saved him a step today. He lowered her onto the sheets, and the grip around his waist pulled him down with her. Here in the bed, her scent was even stronger, enveloping him even as he sat back on his heels and went to work on the snap of her shorts.

The quiver of stomach muscles against the backs of his hands nearly caused his fingers to fumble as desire shot through him. Megan arched, lifting her hips to assist as he slid the last of her clothing off, and his eyes widened.

A small blue butterfly nestled in the hollow beneath her right hip bone.

Megan had a tattoo.

It was beautifully done, this tiny work of art, the detail and shading carefully designed to capture the moment right before flight. The colors contrasted with Megan's fair skin, drawing his fingers like a magnet to smooth over the butterfly's wings.

Seeing it on her body was shocking. And unbelievably arousing.

She hissed softly as he traced the wings, and gooseflesh rose under his seeking fingers, then trembled under his tongue. Capturing his head, she pulled, bringing him level with her body again and meeting his eyes as she worked the snap and zipper of his jeans.

The release brought both pleasure and pain: relief from the confinement mixed with an overwhelming need to bury himself in her. *Now.*

He echoed her earlier hiss of pleasure as she palmed him, and his eyes closed as she stroked him with the practiced ease she'd learned years ago, remembering exactly how to drive him insane.

The pleasure bordered on torment as Meggie fitted into the curve of his body, her leg draping over his and her hips moving restlessly in contrast to the steady stroke of her hand.

He was too close to bear much of her touch, and with a push he flipped her to her back to reacquaint himself with her body.

So many subtle differences, yet it was all so familiar, as well. The faint sprinkle of freckles between her breasts, the indentation of her waist, the long, lean muscle of her thigh… The rediscovery of the curves and planes felt like coming home, only to find something new.

But that wasn't a new feeling either. He hadn't been Megan's first lover, but she'd come to him with only the fumblings of high-school boys forming her experience. Her inherent shyness had masked deep passion waiting to be plumbed, and they hadn't left the bed for nearly two days. Even then, his hands on her skin had felt as if they belonged there, and he'd known...

That memory stirred his blood, but not as much as the gloriously naked woman before him now. This wasn't the same Meggie he'd married, and he was eager to find out who she'd become.

As if she read his mind, Megan's lush lips curled into a seductive smile. Without opening her eyes, she reached for his wrist, stopping his lazy exploration. "You're driving me crazy."

He grinned, knowing she couldn't see it. "That was the plan."

"Touch me, Dev."

The words slammed into him, causing his breath to catch this time. "But I am."

She growled low in her throat, and the frustration fueling the sound rocketed through him like an electric current. "Dev..."

His free hand slid over the butterfly tattoo to her thatch of pale curls, and her thighs opened in welcome. He let his fingers tease gently, enjoying the sight of her hands fisting in the sheets and the sheen of sweat that caused her skin to glisten in the dim half-light of the room. A very un-Meggie-like curse burst from her lips and she finally met his eyes. "Devin!" she demanded, desire choking her words.

"Like this?" he asked as he cupped her sex and felt the heat of her arousal.

Her teeth caught her lip as she tried to press against his hand. He couldn't keep up the game; he needed to feel her. His thumb slipped into the wet heat, and a strangled cry escaped as he found the stiff nub and circled it.

Meggie's response left his hands shaking as he slid one finger inside her body. A moment later her inner muscles gripped him powerfully as she began to tremble from the approaching climax.

Megan was drowning in the sensations, the pleasure Devin's touch brought. The hedonistic side she'd forgotten she had came out in full force, and she wanted more.

She was close, so close to the edge. But she didn't want to go there alone. Not this time. Not after so long. "Dev," she whispered, causing his hooded eyes to meet hers.

He seemed to understand, sliding his big body up to cover hers as he kneed her thighs apart. His weight was welcome, blissful, and she held her breath in anticipation as he sought entrance.

Oh, yes, her body seemed to sigh as he filled her, and she felt her trembles of pleasure echo through Dev's shoulders and arms.

She couldn't hold his stare. It caused her heart to stutter, and she only wanted to enjoy this moment. Closing her eyes, she met his first thrust, and stars burst behind her eyelids.

Then she couldn't think at all. She could only hold on to Dev as the wave took her higher. Vaguely she could hear Dev's breath labor, hear him mumble her name into her hair as he pulled her tightly to him. Dev's arms held her together as she began to shatter, prolonging the pleasure until she felt Dev join her on that precipice.

Devin claimed her mouth in a kiss that scorched her, and Megan exploded in white-hot pleasure as he sent them tumbling over the edge together.

Reality was slow to return, and Megan wasn't encouraging it. She didn't want to have to face the unpleasant thoughts starting to niggle at the edges of her conscience. The dreamy, fuzzy weightlessness of afterglow, the feel of Devin's breath against her neck as it evened out to normal, the lazy sweep of his hand over her hip and thigh… Reality could wait. It would only spoil the moment, and she wanted this moment to last as long as possible.

Forever, something whispered, and she pushed the thought away. She and Devin weren't meant to be forever; she'd learned that the first time. But she was more than willing to enjoy this small interlude from reality without expectation of something more.

She could salve her conscience with the knowledge she was being realistic about *that,* at least.

"Nice tattoo," Dev mumbled against her ear as his fingers traced the butterfly. She'd noticed the way the tattoo had drawn his attention—and his hands and his mouth—repeatedly.

"Thanks." Her voice seemed rusty and thick, but then, so did Devin's. "It hurt like hell getting it, but I love it."

"I never dreamed you'd get a tattoo. You just…"

"Don't seem like the type?" she finished for him. "You and everyone else." Dev stiffened a little for some reason, and his hand stalled briefly on her hip. The moment passed quickly, though, and Megan didn't comment. "The artist in Albany was dating my roommate at the time, so we knew each other a little bit. He did everything to try to talk me out of it, and I think he was surprised when he couldn't."

There was that tension again. Was Dev somehow disapproving of her tattoo? Was that why he was so fascinated by it? "Very talented guy."

"I think so. If you're thinking about getting one yourself, I'll give you his name and number. He'd be worth the trip."

"I'll pass." Dev used his hand to pull her even more snugly against him, and she curled happily into his warmth. "I've heard that's a painful place to get ink."

"Well, I put it on my hip so I can see it but my clients can't. Most people don't think 'Accomplished Professional I Can Tell My Problems To' when they see a tattoo. Regardless of the quality," she added.

"And when did you become a great fan of butterflies?"

Dev knew her, that was for sure. She'd never been a girlie-girl type liking unicorns and butterflies and rainbows. She tried to shrug it off with a casual "It just seemed appropriate at the time."

"Why?"

She hesitated. Her usual response to the few people who knew about her tattoo wouldn't really work now. Not without sounding like a slam against him. "Well," she hedged, "it was about a year after…after…"

"Us?" he supplied.

"Yeah, about a year after us. I had just moved to Albany, and I really felt like I was starting a whole new life. I'd grown and changed so much in that year, I didn't feel I was the same person I used to be."

She felt Devin's nod of understanding, and she worried he'd taken offense. "Transformation," he said.

"It's a trite image, I know. A cliché. But it felt right on the money. And Keith—the artist—understood. He'd watched me come out of my cocoon, but knew I hadn't started to fly yet. That's why he made it look like it's about to take off." She sighed. "It's more about the possibilities that come from change."

A low chuckle rumbled in his chest, and the vibrations moved through her, as well. "Spoken like a shrink."

She elbowed him in response, but it did bring a smile to her face she knew he couldn't see.

Then Devin sobered, his hand pausing on her waist like

a weight. "Regardless of what you may think, I assure you it wasn't my intention to hold you back somehow."

She rolled over and met his eyes. "I know," she said honestly, but Dev frowned at her in disbelief. "At least, I do *now*. Time has given me some perspective. And regardless of what I've said recently, I don't hold you fully responsible for us. I made some mistakes, too."

"The folly and hubris of youth."

"*Hubris?* Did you really just use the word *hubris?*"

Dev propped his head on his fist. "I'm a lawyer. I'm allowed to use arcane words in idle conversation for no good reason."

She shook her head and sighed in censure, but Dev was unmoved and his cheeky grin didn't fade. "Some people hide their insecurities behind big vocabularies, using those big words to make themselves sound superior to others." Dev arched an eyebrow at her and she wanted to smack him. "You're the most arrogant person I've ever met."

"Thank you, Megan."

This was the most comfortable she'd felt around Devin in ages. The barriers between them seemed to have disappeared with their clothes....

Good Lord, she'd never let a client get away with this line of reasoning and kind of rationalizing to excuse their behavior. "You are terrible, Devin Kenney." *And I'm even worse.* "What am I going to do with you?"

A wolfish grin spread across his face, and her heartbeat kicked up in response. Every nerve ending jumped to life at the promise in that grin. "I guess that depends. When do you leave?"

Huh? "I'm sorry? What?"

"On vacation?"

She racked her brain and came up empty-handed. "What

makes you think I'm going somewhere?" *Like I could afford a vacation.*

"The other night you said you needed to pack. For Canada."

"Oh, that." She giggled. "Changing my name and moving to Canada was my backup plan for solving this whole mess."

Dev smirked at her.

"Hey, I was catastrophizing, so it—"

"That's not even a word."

"Yes, it is."

There was that smirk again. "Now who's overcompensating with a big vocabulary?"

She gave in to the urge to smack him. Grabbing the pillow from under her, she swung it at his head. Dev blocked the blow easily, pulling the pillow out of her hand and tossing it to the floor as he wrestled her onto her back and pinned her hands over her head.

Her body reacted instantly, heat pooling in her belly and nipples hardening as Dev settled comfortably between her thighs.

"And now we're back to the earlier topic. What to do…?" Dev's lips found her earlobe and the tiny nibbles sent chills shivering down her body. "Hmm…" The sound vibrated against her throat. "Since you're not going anywhere, I'm thinking I shouldn't either."

Was he planning on staying the night?

"My weekend is free.…"

Weekend? Oh, she knew *that* wasn't a good idea. Giving in to a little ex-sex for old times' sake wasn't uncommon, but a weekend would be—

Her inner hedonist quickly stopped that line of thought, stomping it into oblivion and answering before her brain could regroup. "I don't have any plans."

Dev's smile warmed her heart. But his next words warmed her blood.

"Now you do."

Devin heard his phone beep again, but he wasn't interested in anything other than the woman curled around him.

He ran his hands through the blond strands that snaked across his chest and listened to Megan's even breaths of very deep sleep. The dark circles around her eyes testified to her exhaustion, but considering what had caused that exhaustion...

He smiled as Megan mumbled something in her sleep and shifted.

Sleep, though, escaped him. He should be equally exhausted, but while he was enjoying the bone-deep satisfaction and the languid feeling it brought to his body, he wasn't all that tired. Only the knowledge that Megan *was* kept his hands in her hair and off the rest of her.

Hunger had driven them from bed to order a pizza shortly before ten, and even during their impromptu naked picnic Megan had refrained from discussing any of the reservations he could see written on her face during unguarded moments. He hadn't brought them up either.

It was selfish.

He didn't care.

If there were going to be repercussions or regrets or anything else in the morning, he'd deal with them then. *No,* he amended, *I'll deal with them Monday.* They had the weekend, and he fully intended to keep the world at bay until then. He wasn't going to question whichever of the fates had thrown Megan back into his arms.

He rubbed his fingers over Megan's butterfly again. How such a small tattoo affected him...unreal. From the strange erotic kick it landed on his libido, to the jealousy that flared at the thought of how many men might have been in a position to see it, to the unsettling knowledge that their divorce had, in the end, been such a positive change in Megan's life that she had decided to commemorate it with a permanent mark, that tattoo was seared on his mind.

The tattoo was a very colorful reminder of exactly what this was all about. Any nostalgia awakened in him, any strange ideas that this would—or could—be more were quickly dismissed. This was what it was—nothing more.

Megan stirred, and her arm bumped his. She jumped and sat straight up, pushing her hair out of her face as she turned. The shocked gasp became an embarrassed chuckle. "Sorry. I'm not used to sleeping with someone and when we bumped…" She rubbed a hand across her face to chase the sleep away. "Sorry if I woke you."

Megan sleeps alone. That message was the only one that registered. And for some reason he didn't want to explore—with or without a therapist—he was oddly pleased to hear it. "I wasn't asleep."

"No?" Megan's jaw dropped. "You're not tired? Not after…?"

It was hard to tell in this light, but Megan might have been blushing. "It's barely past midnight, and I'm not that tired."

A wicked grin tugged at Megan's mouth. "That sounds like a challenge." Her hand began to trace over his ribs and stomach, causing him to catch his breath.

"Might be."

"I love a challenge," she said as she lowered her head and swirled her tongue around his navel.

The past few years definitely had wrought changes in Megan.

And he was rapidly coming to appreciate that.

CHAPTER EIGHT

LAST CHRISTMAS, Megan's parents had given her a ladies' tool kit—hammer, screwdriver, pliers, all sized a bit smaller and clad in hot-pink-and-purple polka dots. It had come in handy in this apartment, allowing her to do minor repairs without involving her landlord.

Devin had protested using such girlie tools, and she had to admit that watching him try to put the bathroom door back into its frame with a pink-and-purple screwdriver was quite funny to watch. She perched on the edge of the bathtub, providing unsolicited and unhelpful advice.

"You need real tools," Dev grumbled as he forced a screw back into the frame. The flex and pull of his biceps and shoulders had her full attention, and she was glad he'd not seen the need to put on a shirt while he worked. The small screwdriver slipped, and he cursed. "And a real door in a real apartment. Hand me the hammer."

She stood and her quads lodged a protest at the movement. Her thighs simply weren't used to the level of activity they'd seen last night. And this morning. And this afternoon. "There's nothing wrong with this apartment." Handing him the hammer, she added, "You have no one to blame but yourself for the damage."

That got her a smile that melted her knees. "Really? Who jumped who in the shower?"

She shrugged, trying to seem unaffected by the memory that heated her skin. "But it was your, um, *exuberance* that destroyed my door." The ancient hinges hadn't been able to withstand the force of Dev's thrusts as she was pinned against it.… She cleared her throat. "You break it, you buy it."

"Deal." Dev handed her the tools.

The door still hung at a drunken angle. "Um, hello? Door still not fixed."

"I choose to buy. I'll send a carpenter out here first thing Monday morning." He slipped out behind her, leaving her staring at her broken door.

"Devin…"

He wrapped his arms around her waist from behind, pulling her against his chest. Hard evidence of what Dev would rather be doing pressed against her lower back. "Anyway, there's a good chance we'll break something else before we're done here. Might as well start a running list of repairs—coffee table, bathroom door…" His fingers toyed with the hem of the baggy T-shirt she'd put on shortly after they'd crashed through the bathroom door, snaking under to smooth across her hips and stomach. Her head fell back against his chest as one hand moved up to cup her breast, teasing the nipple to a hard point. Dev's other hand slid lower, those long fingers wringing a moan from her with just a touch.

It was easy, and getting easier, to forget everything that wasn't Devin. The real world seemed like an abstract notion existing only in her mind. Only right now—and only this man—seemed real. Concrete. She was in dangerous territory and going deeper as she angled her neck to give Devin better access to the sweet spot under her ear.

She knew all that. But it was very hard to remember at a moment like this.

Dev was dangerous to her sanity and mental health. His words—*before we're done here*—should have been a reminder that this little interlude from reality wouldn't last. In a way they were a wake-up call, causing a pang in her chest she didn't want to explore.

Because if she did, she'd have to give this up: the magic of Dev's hands on her body, the odd comfort and security she felt just having him here. She didn't want to probe those feelings either.

She just wanted to feel.

As her legs began to tremble and lose the strength to hold her upright, Dev's arm tightened around her, supporting her.

It felt good on so many levels and in so many ways it scared her. Not badly enough to ask Dev to leave, but enough to worry her.

More than her apartment was in danger of getting damaged.

All interludes from reality must come to an end, and something in Dev's sigh and the way he dropped a kiss on the top of her head as he passed told Megan it was time.

They'd been sipping coffee over the remnants of a late Sunday brunch, and between the lengthening periods of silence she couldn't call completely comfortable and the choppy conversation, she'd known it was coming. Hell, she'd known it was coming as she cooked his favorite breakfast frittata for old times' sake this morning. Like so many times before, the frittata had burned due to Devin's ability to distract her. And like so many times before, they'd scraped off the burned bits and eaten it anyway.

It might have seemed like old times, but it wasn't. She knew that. And she was prepared for the words.

"I have to leave soon."

Ouch. Not as prepared as I thought. "I figured."

"I'm doing a morning show in Cincinnati tomorrow and my flight leaves…"

"It's fine, Dev. You have a life. So do I," she lied. "And we should probably get back to them." Proud of how nonchalant she sounded about the situation, she stood and grabbed some dishes off the table. "I'm so far behind on those articles.…"

Devin followed her into the kitchen. "This week's schedule is a nightmare for me. I'm triple booked practically every day."

Let the excuses begin. Was there a phrase book guys got in high school just for the gotta-go-I'll-call-you-sometime moment? "I understand. Just don't forget to send the carpenter, okay?"

A furrow appeared on Devin's forehead. "What's wrong, Megan?"

"You're busy. I get that. You don't need to give me the particulars. I'm just trying to tell you I don't expect anything from you beyond a carpenter to fix my door."

"So that's it?"

"This weekend has been great, but we both know it doesn't mean anything."

Devin actually looked offended at her comment. "I must've missed that memo. I was trying to explain that if you wanted to do dinner—or anything else this week—it would have to be late. After the show."

"Oh." She felt about a foot tall.

Devin's hands closed around her upper arms, and he massaged them lightly. "You know, I'm always advising people to stay away from their exes."

Oh, the irony. "Yeah. Me, too."

The corner of his mouth twitched in amusement. "So neither of us is good at taking our own advice." Then his voice dropped a notch and turned serious. "But I'm not sorry this weekend happened. Are you?"

"Nope. No regrets." *Yet.*

"Then dinner tomorrow night?"

"Okay." A little happy campfire warmed her heart.

Then Dev's kiss fanned the flames, leaving her breathless when he finally broke the kiss with a heartfelt groan. "I wish I didn't have to go."

"Me, too," she admitted as she grabbed the countertop for support.

"I'll call you later." He winked. "Seriously."

Then he was gone, and her apartment felt empty. The tiny rooms seemed bigger now that Dev wasn't filling them, and Megan almost expected them to echo.

As she walked to her bedroom she took stock of the damage they'd done to the apartment: one broken table, one broken door, one lamp that had been kicked off her bedside table. The lamp had survived, but the shade needed to be bent back into shape.

Later, she thought as she crawled back under the covers. Dev's scent still clung to the pillows, and she breathed it deep into her lungs. It was hard to focus on current damage or potential future disasters when caught in residual afterglow.

It had been one crazy week. Not even a full week, she realized after a quick mental count. After years of avoiding everything Devin-related, she'd gone from reading him the riot act on Monday to cuddling his pillow on Sunday. Somehow it seemed like much longer than six days.

Devin just had a knack for turning her life upside down. He always had. Since the day he'd tripped over her step stool in the library stacks and caused her to literally fall into his arms... She smiled at the memory.

And while life with Devin hadn't always been easy, it

had never been dull. It was disconcerting to think how colorless her life had been over the past years. She'd been so focused on one thing that she'd gotten unbelievably boring. Only, she hadn't realized that until Dev had livened up this week considerably.

She should really get up and do something. Work on those articles. Tidy the kitchen. Fix the lampshade. Something other than lie there and obsess over her ex-husband.

But she was warm and comfy and enjoying the obsessing. Which only proved she really was certifiable.

Fate was strange sometimes. Just when she'd thought she had everything all worked out, it had thrown Devin back into the mix. It wasn't an ideal situation—and if she'd ever harbored any wild fantasy about Devin walking back into her life it wouldn't have been like this—but she felt hopeful about the possibilities.

The possibilities that come from change.

The problem, though, was that there was so much change and so many possibilities, it made her head hurt to think about it. That was a lie; it actually made her *heart* hurt to think about it. Because there were so many things that could go horribly wrong.

But there were so many things that could go amazingly right, as well.

She wondered if her apartment would survive the ride....

He'd left Megan's for this? To spend the night alone in a Cincinnati hotel just to get up before dawn to answer the same seven questions he'd answered a hundred times across the country? He had to be insane.

He'd been chafing against the publicity machine for a while now, but tonight drove the point home. This crossed a line into ridiculous. He and Manny and the publicist were going to have a chat about his schedule. It was time to get his life back.

He debated calling Megan just to talk, but he knew she was trying to work on some research she wanted to publish in one of those academic journals. It wouldn't be fair to interrupt her work because he was bored and lonely in Cincinnati.

Especially since he'd kept her from working at all over the weekend. He should feel bad about that, but he didn't. Not in the least.

He could use this time to get some work done, as well. Instead, he pulled the file Simon had passed to him Friday morning.

He'd hired Simon to work part-time last year as a favor to a friend to give the young man some real-world experience before he started law school. Privately, Devin found Simon's zeal a refreshing break from the day-to-day realism of his job, so he always made time when Simon came to him with an interesting case or sticky law to discuss. It kept his brain from atrophying.

But this was different. Simon was moving past theory and discussion of the past and into more current and complicated issues: a local college student's case involving right to privacy, which seemed to be struggling in the system. Simon had copious notes scrawled in the margin of the printout: questions, statute references and a very insightful invoking of the Ninth Amendment to back up his argument.

The kid was sharp. Granted, his reading of the 1969 Supreme Court decision wouldn't hold up long under pressure, but the 1990 decision *would*....

An hour later Devin realized the student in question had one hell of a case but a lawyer who wasn't quite on the ball enough to get it done. And where was the media? Where was the outrage at the blatant disregard of this student's constitutional rights? Why was this flying under the radar?

He booted up his laptop and started sending emails. One to an old classmate who worked for the American Civil Liberties Union now, one to his assistant and one to another radio personality who'd love to break a story like this. That would get everyone started, and by the time he got home tomorrow...

Then he remembered what his schedule for the week was like and grumbled under his breath. He probably didn't have the time to get his hands into something this complicated.

And he knew now that he *wanted* to be in this fight.

Well, he had been planning to make some changes, and this was just more reason to do so. There was no real need for him to continue this junket anyway.

The need to call Megan was really strong now. She'd always been the one to catch the brunt of his enthusiasm. How appropriate he and Megan were back together at the same time he'd found this case. He grinned. Definitely fate trying to tell him something.

But it was late; Megan was probably asleep and he had to be up in a few hours anyway. He'd tell her all about it tomorrow at dinner.

The call had come earlier than expected, but when Megan had seen the clinic's number on her phone she'd known it was over. It hadn't stopped her from hoping, though, that it might work out differently.

At least Julie had called her last night to give her the heads-up so she hadn't been blindsided by it. In the time it had taken to do one search on Google, the rosy afterglow of her weekend and her hopeful outlook had been scrubbed away by internet notoriety and its viral nature.

Dr. Weiss had been calm and measured, never raising her voice as she lectured Megan on professional behavior, privacy issues, the clinic's reputation and bad decision-making. She'd even allowed Megan a chance to explain, raising Megan's hopes before shooting them down in flames.

Then, in that same calm voice, Dr. Weiss had fired her. Megan could come clean out her desk and return her keys after the clinic closed this evening.

Shell-shocked, she'd sat cross-legged on her bed and stared at the phone for a long while, unable to completely process that her career was, for all intents and purposes, over.

But now Megan's pity party was in full swing. Everything she'd worked for was in the toilet, and it wasn't her fault. So she'd acted a little recklessly and made a bad decision, but *this*… This was beyond belief.

Her first response was to blame Devin, but on second thought, this wasn't his style. Plus, after the weekend they'd just shared, she couldn't bring herself to believe Devin would callously sow the seeds to destroy her and then crawl into her bed.

No, this had Kate's manicured fingers all over it. She had to have some kind of personality disorder to do something like this. She wished there was an official diagnosis of Narcissistic Self-Serving Evil Witch Disorder. Antisocial Personality Disorder just didn't seem quite strong enough.

But knowing who to blame didn't change the situation. She was screwed. No matter how she tried to look at it, there was no way to salvage her career. She'd worked so hard in school, fought tooth and nail to get a good internship and now she was at a dead end. Tears burned her eyes and rolled down her cheeks, but they didn't offer any catharsis.

Masochist that she was, she went back to the computer and checked the file on the *Now Hear This* website. She wouldn't torture herself by listening to the clip again, but the counter showed another two hundred clicks in the past hour. Dozens more pingbacks from other sites. The speed of the internet was a dangerous force, but at least she could track the downward spiral of her reputation in real time.

She clicked over to her email to find a message from Devin.

Tried to call, but you're still not answering the phone.

That wasn't entirely true. She'd seen his number on the caller ID, but she didn't trust herself to talk to him at the moment. She might not blame him for this mess, but he was still hip-deep in it.

Still under siege?

That was one word for it.

I'll pick you up after I finish the show. Be thinking about where you want to eat. Oh, and pack a bag. Your place isn't sturdy enough.

Either Dev didn't realize the extent of what that audio clip had done or else he was completely insane. Either way, she didn't plan on leaving the house tonight. She'd go pack up her office as directed, but then she was going back under the covers for a good long wallow in her misery.

Megan debated what to tell Devin. She decided the easiest way out was avoidance. If she confronted him, she'd break down; everything was just too raw right now. Maybe tomorrow she'd feel up to it.

Dev—
Not tonight. Maybe we can talk tomorrow.
M

Megan's short, uninformative email left Devin confused, but since it hadn't arrived until he was about to go on the air, he couldn't follow up. Was she sick?

His intro was playing and he had about four seconds—not enough time to send her an email. He was still planning to go to her place straight from here tonight, and he'd get some answers then, but he'd be left wondering for the next two hours.

He plugged the book, discussed a couple of the celebrity divorce cases making the news, chatted with Kate about upcoming appearances and special guests, but he couldn't shake the uneasy feeling something wasn't right with Megan.

But the listener queue was growing, and Kate was connecting his first caller. He needed to get his mind back on what he was doing.

Thankfully, none of the first few callers had complicated or sticky problems. Devin could fall back on stock answers, recited from memory. Oddly, the question he'd been expecting didn't come until just before the first break.

"So where's Dr. Megan tonight?"

"Living her life, saving marriages, that kind of thing." He tried to sound friendly and casual about it. "She might come back and visit at a later date, but this isn't exactly her area of expertise." He laughed. "Or interest, for that matter. What can I help you with?"

"My ex-wife is about as psycho as yours, but my ex has no problem pulling out the crazy in public."

Psycho?

"So what I want to know is how you manage to keep that crazy under control in front of other people. I don't care what she says to me, but I'm tired of having an audience. You two were fine on the show last week, so how'd you get her to act normal?"

This wasn't the question he'd been expecting. He looked at Kate for confirmation this caller was off his rocker. Her shrug and grin set alarm bells ringing.

He chose his words carefully. "If your ex is truly mentally ill—"

"No, just bitchy like yours."

"Excuse me?"

The caller laughed. "Dude, we all heard the clip. I give you major props for keeping your cool the way you did, 'cause *damn*—"

Devin was missing a piece of the puzzle, but thanks to the caller, he now had a clue where to find it. He disconnected the call. "Caller? You there? Kate? We seem to be having some technical difficulties. I've lost the caller."

Kate looked at her board. "I'm not sure what happened.…" She looked up, saw his signal and nodded in understanding. "Sorry, folks, something's weird here. We're going to go to break while I sort it out."

While Kate scrambled, Devin was already typing in the URL to the website where Kate uploaded what she called his "greatest hits"—the craziest or funniest or most ridiculous calls. It didn't take him long to see which clip was getting the most traffic: "Behind the Scenes with Devin and Dr. Megan." The counter showed thousands of listens, and the comment tail…

"Okay, we went to tape." Kate's voice came through the studio's speakers. "What's going on?"

His anger was simmering already, so he ignored her as he clicked play. Ten seconds later he understood the caller's words. Ten seconds after that, he knew why Megan wasn't in the mood for dinner.

And the clip was five and a half minutes long. His blood was boiling by the one-minute mark.

Kate was lucky she was on the other side of the glass and not where he could get his hands on her immediately. She might have killed the live feed on their mics the other night, but the ratings-chasing bitch had kept the recording going. With a little splicing and dicing, Kate had turned his and Megan's private, off-air discussions into a juicy sound clip, totally distorting what actually happened. Thanks to Kate's editing, Megan did sound a bit like a psycho.

"Take it down." Kate opened her mouth to argue, but he wasn't interested. "Take it down *now.*"

She pressed her lips into a thin line, but turned to her computer. A few seconds later she nodded, and when he refreshed the page, the clip was gone.

"It's still out there, you know. The internet never forgets."

"Then you'd better get busy on some kind of retraction or apology."

"Devin," she argued through the glass separating them, "it's been the number-one clip on *Now Hear This* since Saturday morning. It's viral and people can't get enough of it—or you. The hits to your site have gone through the roof. Your book is number one on Amazon today."

Kate's blindness to anything that couldn't be ranked, rated or re-tweeted had never been so clear. Or so dangerous. She might not care about people, but she definitely cared about her job. He targeted his comment to that care. "Are you *trying* to get us sued?"

Kate shrugged. "Megan has no grounds to sue us for anything. She agreed to be on the show. She agreed to be taped and possibly used for promotional purposes."

"She didn't agree to have you edit her words into something damaging to her reputation, though. Somewhere there's an attorney trying to get her to sue even as we speak."

"Good! Let her sue. The added publicity—"

He leaned close to the microphone and spoke carefully. "You're fired."

"What?"

"You heard me."

"We're in the middle of a show, Devin."

"I'll handle it."

Kate turned mutinous, crossing her arms over her chest. "I work for this station, not you. You can't fire me."

"Exactly who do you think this station values more? Me or the person who answers my phone?"

That statement hit home and Kate turned an unflattering shade of angry red. "You son of a…" Her eyes narrowed. "I made this show a hit, you know."

"Then you won't have any problem finding someone else to work for. But you no longer work on *my* show."

Kate tossed her headphones on the desk as Devin opened the door between the booths. "Go to hell, Devin Kenney."

She flounced out the door past him, leaving a trail of expensive perfume in her wake. He had no doubt he'd hear from the studio's Powers That Be in the morning, pleading her case.

He'd produce his own damn show before he had her back in the booth again.

Speaking of, his show was currently running on tape and the listeners had to be confused.

Sliding into Kate's chair, he paused the tape and pulled the mic close. "Sorry, folks, but we're having major technical difficulties this evening. Must be the full moon or something. Apologies to everyone on hold and out there listening, but we're going to have to rely on some old favorites for the rest of tonight's show."

Oh, he'd be hearing about this tomorrow, too, but right now he had bigger tigers to tame.

Down the hall he found one of the sound techs messing with some ad spots. "Do you know how to run a board?"

The young man nodded.

"Good. Babysit my show, will you?"

Devin waited only long enough for the shocked tech to nod again before he continued on. With *Cover Your Assets* covered, he dialed Manny's number as he waited for the elevator.

"Devin! Great show tonight. You were fab, as always...."

Manny's butt-kissing grated his last nerve. "The show is still on, you jackass. Why didn't you tell me Kate had posted some hatchet-job clip on the web?"

"Because you told me not to call you until noon today, and by then it was old news." Manny's sniff said he wasn't over that insult. "But the good news is that your book has jumped to number one on Amazon."

Damn. What kind of idiots had he surrounded himself with? "You'd better come up with a stellar form of damage control for this."

"Devin, you have nothing to worry—"

"For *Megan,* you fool. Could you think beyond your fifteen percent for just a minute?" The elevator started its descent to the parking garage. "You and Kate have the ethical standards of mob bosses."

"Kate and I only want to do what's best for you and your career. And look! You're the hottest thing right now."

"And Kate is looking for a new job." He waited for Manny to connect the dots to the precarious position he was in at the moment.

"Look, I know you and Megan are revisiting your younger years, and you're feeling all nostalgic and lovey-dovey after your weekend…"

How does Manny know where I'd spent the weekend? Damn tabloids.

"But, Devin, you have a public image to uphold. A persona you've created that you have to honor for your fan base."

"I'm an attorney. My public image can't be 'screw everyone over.' Do you even know what the term *ethical* means?"

"Your fans don't see you as an attorney."

"Then you definitely have some major work ahead of you fixing *that* situation." Manny started to sputter something again, and Devin cut him off. The elevator doors opened, and Devin was nearly at his car. "We will talk tomorrow about future plans for my career and public image. In the meantime, you need to get busy with your spin machine and generate some pushback."

Not waiting for Manny's agreement, Devin hung up and cranked the engine. He looked at his phone, then tossed it in the passenger seat. No sense calling Megan now; she wouldn't answer and he'd be there in a few minutes anyway.

He'd lost control over a large part of his life without realizing it, and this was his wake-up call.

CHAPTER NINE

As Devin parked in front of Megan's apartment, a feeling of dread settled in his stomach. At least a dozen photographers had set up camp in front of Megan's—drawing an interested crowd of neighbors to gawk at the circus. They converged on him before the car came to a complete stop, turning the short trip up to her building into a gauntlet of shouted questions and flashbulbs.

He didn't doubt the crowd had a lot to do with Megan's earlier message. His fault or not, there was a very good chance Megan blamed him for this latest fiasco. If she'd been *trying* to become the most infamous ex in Chicago, his people couldn't have done a better job achieving it for her. No wonder she didn't want to see him tonight. Had she been dealing with this all day?

He knocked on the door, calling her name so she'd know it was him and not another tabloid looking for a story. Then he held his breath. Moment-of-truth time. Would she even open the door? If she didn't, they'd both be fodder for the tabloids tomorrow.

Megan opened the door, but she didn't look overly happy to see him. She was pale, with dark half-moons under her eyes as if she hadn't slept last night, and he knew Kate—and by extension, he, too—was to blame. "Dev, I—"

"Kate's evil. I had no idea what she'd done until half an hour ago."

"I believe you." She sounded sincere, but she didn't open the door wider and invite him in.

"I fired her." Megan's eyebrows rose in shock. "And I have Manny at work on damage control even as we speak. I'm sorry about this."

Megan nodded, accepting his apology, and her lips pressed into a line as she seemed to weigh it against the damage already done.

"You have to let me in. Otherwise we'll be on every gossip blog in minutes."

"You think we won't be anyway?" She sounded disgusted, but she stepped back and held the door open for him.

First major hurdle cleared. But Megan kept plenty of distance between them as she closed the door and crossed to the couch on the other side of the room. Changing her mind, she took the chair instead, presumably to keep him from joining her on the couch. *So, the cold barrier circling Megan like a razor-wire fence will be my next challenge.* Before he could decide how to approach her, though, he noticed the four boxes next to the door. Boxes that hadn't been there yesterday when he left. That didn't bode well. "What's all this? Still planning that trip to Canada?" he joked.

Megan's humorless laugh chilled him. "I wish. Those would be the contents of my office. Kate isn't the only one who lost her job today over this."

What? "You got fired?"

She braced her elbow on the arm of the chair and propped her chin on it. "You sound surprised."

"Well, *yeah.* Some stupid audio clip makes the internet rounds and you lose your job?" He claimed the corner of the couch closest to her chair. "That's insane." But it did explain much more about her attitude and the pinched look around her eyes.

"No, that's what happens when you work in a profession where discretion is paramount and reputation is everything. My lack of the first has destroyed the second." The even cadence and tinge of sarcasm made him think that might have been a direct quote from her boss.

"The clip has been removed."

She nodded. "I appreciate that, but the damage is done."

"So you get another job, start rebuilding your reputation.…" He trailed off as Megan shook her head. "Why not?"

"I guess I didn't explain this clearly the other night. Internships are really hard to come by. Good ones are even more competitive." She leaned back with a sigh as she continued. "Internships paying a decent wage are few and far between, and unless I want to starve and default on my student loans, I'm not in a position where I could work at one of the nonpaying ones, even if there was one available. There's no place for me to go to rebuild my reputation." She snorted. "Not that it matters now."

Megan had to be overreacting—nothing was unfixable— but considering the day she'd had, he wouldn't call her on it now. "Why?"

"Dr. Weiss isn't the only one concerned with the reputation of her clinic. No reputable therapist is going to hire an intern who's been outed on the internet with borderline personality disorder."

"But you don't. That was all Kate, and she's going to admit it in public."

"Yeah, well, a retraction won't spread nearly as wide or as quickly, and it will still sound fishy to anyone hiring."

She sighed. "And even if I could find someone to hire me and let me finish my hours, the state licensing board isn't going to be impressed. They do background checks, you know. This mess has brought everything—my abilities, my education, my ethics, even my mental stability—into question. Even if they could look past the fact I was fired from an internship, do you think the state is going to grant a license to the infamous and possibly crazy Dr. Megan?"

She was obviously hurting, but... "There are plenty of doctors far more infamous than you. Who's the one with the TV show?"

Calmly—almost too calmly—Megan shook her head. "They got their licenses before they became famous. Most of them don't have licenses now because they weren't able to get them renewed. But there's no requirement that they need one to do those kinds of shows, so..."

He could strangle Kate, but he also had to admit he wasn't fully innocent either. He hadn't known what the repercussions could be, and he hadn't torpedoed her career intentionally, but he definitely shared the blame. "So what do we do?"

"*We* don't do anything. Tomorrow *I* will go find a job—"

"Good. Where?"

She shrugged. "I can tend bar, wait tables..."

With her skills? "You have a PhD."

"So do a lot of other people. You'd be surprised at the educational levels of the folks serving your dinner. Just one of many reasons to tip your servers well—they probably have enormous student loan debt." Her attempt at humor fell flat, and her wan smile told him she knew it, too.

"This is ridiculous. Kate is going to confess that she doctored the clip. If anyone is going to look bad, it's her.

Manny is working his spin right now. And if you need money—"

"You'll loan it to me?" she scoffed.

"Forget loan." She stiffened, and he looked for a non-insulting way to give her the money. "Manny has been quick to tell me how much I'm making off this fiasco, so it's fair to say you've earned it."

She shook her head again. For someone who seemed to be on the edge of disaster, she was oddly calm and rational. "Dev, I'm not looking for a sugar daddy. I'll figure something out."

Stubborn woman. "Why won't you let me help you?"

"Because my problems are not your problems."

It sure felt like it, though. He tried to inject some humor. "Just last week you said I was the source of your problems."

A small smile tugged at her cheek. "True."

"Then let me help you get through this."

She fell silent and the beginnings of the smile faded. He recognized the look on Megan's face. She was having an interesting internal debate, coming to a decision about something. He just wasn't sure which decision about what. A long moment later, Megan took a deep breath. He braced himself.

"I kind of got the impression when you left yesterday— and correct me if I'm wrong—that this past weekend was some sort of new start for us. Was I wrong about that?"

The brutal honesty in her words caught him off guard. Whatever he'd prepared himself for, that wasn't it.

Asking Devin that question had taken all the bravado she could muster. The look of shock he wore now made her want to take the question back. *No, it's a fair question. I jumped into bed with him again, so I have a right to know what he's thinking this is about.* Megan ignored the obvious addendum that she should have asked that *before* they had sex.

Don't back down. She straightened her spine. "Well, Dev?"

Devin cleared his throat. "Is that what you want?"

"Don't play games. I'm not expecting you to drop to your knees and propose or anything. I just need to know if this is fun and games for old times' sake or if there's a possibility this might go somewhere. Eventually."

A long moment passed and her heart began to stutter in her chest. Had she read this situation all wrong? "I told you I have no expectations of you, but I think it might be helpful to be sure we're on the same page."

Dev nodded. "There's always a possibility, right?"

That wasn't exactly a ringing endorsement of any future, but considering their past… No, she couldn't hide behind Devin again now. She'd worked too hard to make something of herself, to be someone other than just Devin's wife. She couldn't do it. Not now. "Then there's no way I can take money from you."

That brought Dev's irritation back to the forefront. He pushed to his feet and began to pace. "That makes no sense at all, Megan."

"As you noted before, I'm a different person from the one you used to know. I've worked hard, and there's no way I can go into any, ahem, 'possibilities' as anything less than an equal. If I let you play knight-with-a-big-fat-wallet then we're not equals."

"So you'll accept nonfinancial help? Like if I put Manny to work?"

"Only if Manny wants to sign me as a client, too."

Dev rubbed a hand over his face in exasperation. "You're being ridiculous."

"And you're being overbearing." She caught herself and

tamped down her temper. "Try to see this from my point of view. If I'm ever going to salvage my career, then I need to salvage my pride first."

Dev shook his head and snorted. "You're wrong."

It was getting much more difficult to keep her ire under control. "Excuse me?"

"If you want to salvage your career, you're going to have to swallow your pride. Your ego is bruised and your feelings are hurt, but—"

What the…? "Hang on, which one of us is the shrink?"

"This has nothing to do with psychology. This is PR, and I understand the circus you're caught in better than you do. Forget about your pride for the moment. Do whatever you have to do to get through this and your pride will recover with your career."

"You talk a good game, Dev, but—"

"No buts. How do you think my clients get through ugly public divorces where all of their dirty little secrets make the papers and still have careers on the other side?"

He had a point. And he knew she knew it. She could tell by the smirk on his face. "Fine. I'll bite. What do you suggest?"

He stood in front of her and crossed his arms over his chest. "Now that you don't have to worry about your boss, take control of your press. For real this time."

She waved the advice away. "This from the person who doesn't even read his own press." When Dev continued to stare at her expectantly, she elaborated. "I tried that already, remember? It's why this is worse, not better."

"Meggie, Meggie, Meggie." Dev shook his head sadly. "You went into it with the wrong attitude. Now, go put on a dress."

"Are you bipolar now? Why would I do that?"

"Because we're going to dinner. That's the first step in discrediting Kate's little hatchet job. Plus, I'm hungry."

"I'm not in the mood to go out." Even to her own ears she sounded like a petulant five-year-old.

"Tough." Devin leaned forward and placed his hands on the arms of the chair, effectively caging her. He let his eyes roam down her body in a way that left her wiggling slightly in her seat. "As much as I'd rather stay in, you need to be out in public. You need to give that crowd out front a picture of you with your head held high and going on with your life. Right now you're acting like you've done something to be ashamed of, and they'll feed on that. Anyway, you're going to need the energy a good, well-balanced meal provides," he promised with a wicked grin.

Her career was in tatters and she'd spent the day wallowing in it without ever coming up with a solution. She didn't necessarily believe Devin's plan would work, but it was still nice to have a plan. To have someone in her corner staying optimistic—not with "tomorrow is another day" platitudes, but with actual plans—when she couldn't. "Okay. I'll get dressed."

Devin grinned and leaned in for a kiss that lingered long enough to shake the last of the sluggishness off and bring her body to life. And when Dev offered her a hand to help her to her feet, she realized how much lighter she felt. How odd. Today was the worst day of her life, but it didn't seem insurmountable anymore.

Something was terribly wrong with her. This feeling, though...

Megan didn't let go of the hand pulling her out of the chair. She twined her fingers through his instead and tugged him closer. Based on their history, she and Dev probably weren't a good idea, and getting more involved with him now was an even worse one, but with her road map and game plan totally shot to hell, she had nothing but possibilities ahead of her.

Devin was one she was willing to explore.

Dev's eyes lit as she slid her other hand over his chest to his neck, pulling his head closer to hers. "Before I get dressed, I need to get undressed, and if I'm getting undressed…"

She didn't get to finish the statement. Or the thought. Or any thoughts for a long *wonderful* while.

Years ago, Megan had worshipped Dev. His strength, his passion, his charisma—in her eyes, he'd been just a rung down from deity. Over the next week, though, she began to wonder if Dev had moved up the celestial ladder while she hadn't been looking.

Devin spoke; people listened. He wanted something done; it got done. He had minions and assistants and interns at his beck and call. He had hangers-on and yes-men genuflecting and seeking his approval or support.

He could walk into any restaurant and immediately get a table. Random strangers in a bar would send drinks to him or pick up the tab. He played poker with the mayor and golf with the governor's son. She half expected to find he had the president on speed dial.

She'd known he was famous. She'd known he was popular. She just hadn't realized how popular and famous and rich and influential he was.

And it bothered her a little bit. More than a little bit.

The reasoning behind her unease didn't hold up under close scrutiny because Devin didn't seem overly affected by it. Aside from his disparaging comments about her apartment, of course. When she called attention to it, he'd just shrug and brush it off as being the nature of the business. This attitude worked—at least for him—but Megan still felt uncomfortable in the spotlight. Granted, it was Devin's spotlight and she just happened to be sharing it, but that light illuminated all the problems and inequalities and potential issues in getting involved....

And it gave her an excuse, however flimsy and annoying Dev found it to be, to continue to return to her own apartment on a regular basis. As she was now.

Only one photographer waited for her this morning—down from four at the start of the week—so she smiled and waved as she climbed the steps.

The blogs had a field day with their public reconciliation, just as Dev had predicted, especially coming so quickly on the heels of Kate's disastrous—and now discredited—audio clip. Another appearance on Dev's show, several very public dinners and a few pictures of her leaving Dev's building in the early-morning hours had the media buzzing in a whole new direction. She'd gone from "psycho ex" to "the woman who might tame Devin Kenney" in a matter of days. Dev had been right about that much.

But she still didn't have a job or a plan for what she'd do next. The focus of the media attention had turned positive, which was nice on a personal level, but the attention was still there. No job meant no money, and she couldn't float for long on her meager savings. She couldn't—wouldn't—allow Dev to give her money, so something had to give one way or the other.

That was a more solid reason behind her return to her apartment every day. She and Dev might be "exploring possibilities," but there was no sense in getting used to Dev's fancy condo on Lakeshore Drive or the limos or the box seats. Coming back to her place kept her from getting too complacent, reminding her nothing right now was permanent.

It also reaffirmed her commitment to not get into anything

serious while they were on such different playing fields.
She'd done that before, and look how that had ended
up....

No, she and Dev were having a good time, healing some
old wounds and burying some ghosts from the past. That
was healthy. That was positive. The fact it was repairing
some damage to her ego and professional image was also
a plus.

But she refused to read anything else into it.

She also *had* to find a job. Megan dropped her bag onto
the couch and logged on to her email to see if she had any
responses to the feelers she had out.

At the core of all this was the uncertainty, and that
uncertainty was getting to her. Too much was up in the air
for her to feel comfortable about anything. Her "possibilities that come from change" line wasn't at all comforting,
and she was beginning to think it was the stupidest mantra
she'd ever adopted. Much less tattooed on her body.

Her email in-box had plenty of messages, but none of
any help. However, against her better judgment and over
Manny's protests, Devin had put Manny to work on her
behalf, and Manny's name in the return address of one
message caught her attention.

Sorry, Megan. No one is biting. Honestly, you're
just not as interesting now that you and Devin are
a couple.

Being pronounced uninteresting stung a bit, but all
things considered, that wasn't unexpected. Manny's casual
use of "couple" to describe her and Devin, however, *was*.
Some blogs had speculated about their possible couple-ship,
mainly because Divorce Attorney and Marriage Counselor
Reconcile made interesting headlines, but Manny?

No. Manny is just quoting public feeling about my uninteresting self, that's all.

But this was ridiculous. As she expected, she was too notorious to land another internship with any reputable clinic, and the amount of time she had to get her internship hours completed if she still planned to sit the licensing exam anytime soon was ticking away. Her first instinct on that was proving correct. The irony was kicking her, because now she wasn't notorious enough to get a job providing even weak psychotainment for the masses.

It was frustrating. Annoying. Scary. Normally, any one of those things would have her scuttling to get out and restore order to her universe. The only thing unnerving her now was her tepid response and inability to get overly worked up over it. She could blame—or was it credit?—the Dev-caused endorphins for the lack of overachiever response this should be causing.

Speak of the devil… Dev's ring tone sounded from the depths of her bag.

"Where are you, Meggie?"

"Home."

"I just tried that number. Why didn't you pick up?" He sounded distracted.

She sighed. "*My* home, Dev. Not yours."

"Why do you insist on going back there every day? My place is plenty big enough—"

"We've had this conversation, Dev," she interrupted, and heard his exasperated sigh. "So what's up?" Clicking her email client closed, she set the computer on the coffee table and leaned against the cushions.

"Crazy day and I left a file in the kitchen.…"

"Yeah, I saw one when I went to make coffee."

"I was hoping I could convince you to bring it to me."

She could hear the wheedle in his voice. "I'll take you to lunch after."

Drive back to Dev's, get the file, drive to his office... It would be way past lunchtime by the time she got there. She looked around. It wasn't as if she had much of anything else to do today. "I guess I could do that."

"I appreciate it. See you in a little while."

She hadn't even had a chance to take off her shoes. She grabbed her keys and bag, locked the door and waved at the photographer again on her way out.

Halfway to Devin's she remembered his army of assistants and minions. Why didn't he send one of them to his apartment to get the file if it was so important? It would have been quicker and easier for everyone.

The next thought sent a chill through her veins. He was treating her like his wife again. And not in a good way. Belatedly she realized she'd set herself up for this exact thing—doing some cooking, running a different errand for him yesterday on her way home. They'd fallen back into some older habits, so why was she surprised about this one? After all, why send an assistant to do a job your wife could do—and had done—hundreds of times? What was next? Picking up his dry cleaning?

Talk about unequal playing fields...

Oh, no. This did not bode well at all.

The receptionist buzzed Devin to let him know Megan was on her way to his office. He looked at his watch. *That was quick.* Good. He could give the file back to Simon and send him over to meet with Mark from the ACLU. As soon as the publicity junkets surrounding his book ended—and he had Manny working on that—he'd be able to devote some time to this young man's case. Until then, Simon would get some real-life experience being Devin's assistant in the preliminaries.

He called out when he heard Megan's knock. She'd been curled up under the covers when he left this morning, mumbling about catching up on her sleep. The stress was getting to her, he knew. The job hunt was going nowhere, she was worried about money and the state licensing exam, and even the adjustment of the media's attitude hadn't been able to lift that from her shoulders. She had a good game face, but he knew her too well.

If she'd just accept his help... No, Megan seemed determined to dig in her heels and go it alone. It was a bit insulting when he thought about it. She'd play his arm candy for the press, and she happily warmed his bed and body in the evenings, but she had a concrete wall around her that he couldn't breach when it came to anything more.

There was a pinched look on her face when she stuck her head around the door, and he knew not only had there not been any developments in the search for another internship, something else had gone wrong, as well.

"You okay?" he asked, knowing he probably wouldn't get a real answer.

"Great. Here's the file you left. And another one I found on the coffee table. I wasn't sure if you needed it."

"Thanks, Meggie. You're a lifesaver." She accepted the light kiss he pressed against her lips, but didn't respond otherwise. "Let me give this to Simon and I'll take you out for a quick bite to eat."

"I'm not hungry. Thanks anyway."

Oh, he knew that tone. He leaned against the desk. "Okay, what's wrong?"

"Nothing."

He waited.

"I'm not your lackey. Next time you need your errands run, ask one of your assistants."

"I didn't realize it would be an inconvenience—"

"Because I don't have a job?" she challenged.

That might have figured into his request a small bit, but only a fool would admit that now. Not with Meggie getting her dander up already. "Would you believe it was an excuse to get you to come down here and have lunch with me?" That was true as well, and wouldn't give Meggie a reason to hand him his head.

"No, but you get points for trying."

"You could've said no if you were busy."

"I think we've established I'm not busy," she grumbled. "I just don't think we should be falling back into any old habits one or both of us might resent."

She'd been practicing that statement. And while he could tell Megan might not actively be looking for a fight, the set of her shoulders told him she wouldn't back down from one either. "Next time I'll send someone, okay?"

"Thank you." Her shoulders relaxed. "Now you can buy me lunch."

That was a turnaround. "So you're hungry after all?"

"Maybe."

"Are we playing some kind of game?"

"No games." She cocked an eyebrow at him. "I think we're both a little old for that, don't you?"

"And we know each other a little too well for it to work."

Megan smiled. "That, too." She pointed at the file. "I assume that's the case you were telling me about?"

He nodded. Poor Megan had had to listen to his lecture on the privacy doctrine and the Fourteenth Amendment for an hour the other night. And she'd done so wearing nothing but a sheet and a smile he hadn't seen since he'd done the same thing in law school. "I'm sending Simon over to the ACLU office today."

"It's nice to see you so excited about this."

He *was* excited. It was an unusual feeling. "It's been a while, that's for sure."

"But there are only so many hours in the day. When will you have time for it all? Your practice, the show, the book and now this."

"Some things are going to be rearranged in the future." He took the file to the hallway and waved down a paralegal with instructions to find Simon. Then he closed the door carefully behind him, making sure it latched. "I've been so caught up in show business—both mine and my clients'—I forgot I was a lawyer."

"Good for you, Dev. This kid is very lucky—your smarts will help the case, but your name recognition will help, too."

"Well, it definitely won't hurt." He leaned against the desk. "The media seems to have ignored this case, but…"

She perched on the edge of his desk, as well. "But we know what happens to anyone who gets in your orbit. Instant headlines." The small laugh Megan finished with couldn't mask the dry tone.

"Do you regret being back in my orbit?"

"No." She looked at him sideways and smiled weakly. "Well, maybe a little," she corrected. "I wish I hadn't lost my job over it, but being with you again…"

He waited as she thought.

"Honestly? Hmm, well, being with you doesn't suck, either." The hand on the desk slid over to close around his.

It wasn't exactly the enthusiastic response his ego had hoped for, but he'd take it. A small tug was all it took to pull Megan into his arms, and she rose on her tiptoes to capture his lips with hers.

Megan's kiss, whether she meant it to be carnal or not, instantly heated his blood. His hands tightened on her waist, pulling her closer, fitting her body to his.

Her shirt wasn't tucked in, and it was easy to slide his hand under the hem to find soft, warm skin. Megan jumped and broke away. "Dev! Someone could—"

"No one will."

She gasped as he released the clasp of her bra, then sighed as his hands cupped her breasts. "I didn't come here for a nooner on your desk," she protested weakly.

"Okay," he said, then nearly laughed at the disappointed look on her face. He levered himself off the desk and led her to the other side of his office. "However, as you'll notice, shrinks aren't the only ones with couches in their offices."

CHAPTER TEN

"HAVE YOU TRIED CALLING Dr. Kincaid's clinic?" Julie brought Megan a glass of wine and tried a little too hard to sound upbeat. "I hear…" She trailed off when Megan shook her head.

"I've tried *everyone*. No one will touch me with a ten-foot pole. Well," she amended, "Dr. Hearst at that clinic in Elgin seemed interested, but he's a bit of a quack. And I got the feeling he wanted to…" She couldn't finish.

"Wanted to what?"

"Touch me."

"Ew." Julie shuddered slightly.

"Tell me about it."

"What can I do?" The concern was genuine. Julie had gone above and beyond Megan's expectations in trying to help. First by advocating with Dr. Weiss, then by sending out requests to her contact list to see if anyone needed an intern. Julie hadn't had any more luck than Megan herself.

"You've done everything you can, and I'm very appreciative. So this—" she indicated the wine and snacks "—is exactly what I need. Girl talk. Drinks without the sympathy. A chance to just hang out."

"*Mi casa, su casa.*" Julie's eyes turned sympathetic anyway. "And that can be literal, if necessary."

"I'm not in danger of being evicted. Yet." But it was still nice to know she had a place to go if it came to that. Julie's apartment was a castle compared to hers, but then, Julie's family was more well-off and she was still on their payroll. Megan didn't want to go to her parents for help just yet, even though they'd offered, because she wasn't willing to admit defeat. "Actually, I called one of my professors and he's got a possible lead for me."

"Really? That's great."

"It's a small clinic with low-income clients, and I'd be doing mostly substance-abuse work."

"I hear a *but,*" Julie said.

"But the money is tiny. And it's in Carbondale."

The wrinkle in Julie's nose said a lot. "That's like, what? Four hours from here?"

"Five and a half." She tried to sound enthusiastic. "But the cost of living would be a lot less, so if I picked up a part-time job on the side, I might be able to make it work."

Julie looked over the edge of her wineglass. "What did Devin have to say about this?"

"I haven't told him anything about it yet. He doesn't understand why I don't just move into his place as it is."

"Honestly, neither do I."

"Jules, would you move back in with your ex-husband?"

"I don't have an ex-husband."

"Touché. But moving in with Dev isn't a great idea." At Julie's doubtful look, she added, "Aside from obvious benefits, of course. Just because we lived together before, that doesn't mean we should be rushing right back into it. Anyway—" she took a long drink of her wine "—I'm not sure where Dev and I are heading at the moment, and I don't think he is either. Even if I did have an idea, it's still not an option."

"Why not?"

She couldn't stop the pitiful tone that crept into her voice. "Because I'd feel like I'd failed at my own life and gone crawling back to him."

"So you'd rather move away?"

"No, but at least I'd be succeeding or failing on my own."

"You were succeeding just fine until Devin's career intersected with yours so disastrously. This isn't a failure, and even if it was, it wouldn't be your fault."

"I know. But if I let Dev ride to my rescue, I'll never get my feet back under me. It would be like I hadn't accomplished anything over the last seven years, because I'd just be Meggie again. I can't do it. I *won't* do it."

Julie looked at her oddly. "Is there something you haven't told me about your marriage?" she asked cautiously.

"It's nothing like what you're thinking." She drank deeply from her glass while she tried to find the right words. "Part of what drove us apart was that I was just 'Devin's wife.' He might not have been *the* Devin Kenney back then, but he wasn't much different than he is now. Popular. Important. On a smaller scale, of course, but still… I always felt like the sidekick—and not even a useful sidekick with my own superpowers and cool toys. More like the useless one you feel sorry for and can't understand why the hero puts up with them. I can't live the rest of my life as the sidekick."

"It doesn't have to be like that. I didn't know you then, but I know you now, and you definitely aren't just a sidekick."

"Thanks." She fiddled with her glass some more. "Then, of course, there's also the very real possibility Dev and I could fall apart again. I can't risk my future on…on…on whatever this is we're doing."

"*Is* that a possibility?"

"Anything's a possibility, but think about it, Dr. Moss. What do you think our chances are? Realistically."

Julie frowned.

Megan swirled the wine in her glass. "Exactly. Reuniting with your ex is all about remembering why you got together in the first place."

"And the hot sex."

Megan rolled her eyes. "I never should have told you that. Yes, there's fabulous hot sex, but I know better than to assume anything about any kind of future based on the hotness of the sex. You and I both know the problem with reunions is that all the reasons you broke up are usually there, too, lurking beneath the surface, just waiting to blow the whole thing to hell again."

"But you know all the lurking problems, so…"

"If I was your client, would you be encouraging this?"

"Probably not." Julie leaned over to refill both glasses. "But you're not my client. You're Dr. Megan." She lifted her glass in a mock toast.

"I can't tell you how much I hate that name and what it implies."

"Don't be such a snob. So four or five months in Carbondale, huh?" Julie shuddered delicately.

"You make it sound like I'm being exiled to Siberia. Carbondale isn't the ends of the earth."

"But it's not Chicago, either."

"It may take a crowbar to get you *out* of the city, but I'm a bit more flexible. Six months, tops, and I'll be back. Plus, there's the added perk of giving all of this time to really die down and be forgotten. I'll come back, get my license and we can start our own practice just like we planned. Only with one small detour."

"You sound like your mind is made up."

"Almost. I can't dither around with this. The clinic needs someone ASAP and I need a job ASAP. Something has to happen soon."

"Which brings me right back to my earlier question. What about Devin?"

Megan didn't have a ready answer. Julie, good counselor that she was, sat quietly and patiently while Megan thought. "I've made a lot of decisions in my life where Devin was a weight on the scale. I moved to Urbana for him so he could go to law school, then I moved to Albany in spite of him. I'll admit Devin is one of the factors in this equation, but I really need to make this decision based on what *I* want and what's best for *me* in the long term."

"And that is…?"

Megan took a deep breath and blew it out noisily. "I wish to God I knew."

Megan was being uncharacteristically quiet tonight. She'd been getting less talkative for two days now, but had lapsed into almost complete silence tonight. Something was up, but Devin knew he wasn't any more likely to get an answer now than he had been yesterday or the day before.

But she was here, at least. She wouldn't stay at his place full-time, but she was spending more time here than at her apartment these days, so she might be coming around to the idea. It was progress.

Megan was curled up on one end of the couch watching the news while he stretched out with his laptop on the opposite end. They'd fallen back into what Megan used to call "old married people mode" as if they'd never been apart. It was familiar and oddly pleasant, and for the first time in a long time he'd started looking forward to his evenings off. He even found himself looking for ways to clear his schedule to have more free time and actually have a life again.

So he was content to wait for her to talk. Whatever was going on inside her head, it couldn't be his fault, or he knew she wouldn't be here. *She might,* he amended, *but she wouldn't be silent about it.* He'd be getting an earful if it was his fault, so he knew the best approach to Megan's silence was to wait it out until she was ready to talk.

As if she heard his thoughts, Megan turned off the TV and nudged him with her foot. "I got offered a job. A chance to finish out my internship almost on schedule."

He set the laptop aside. "That's great, Meggie. I told you you'd find one. There's a bottle of champagne still in the fridge...." He trailed off when she shook her head, and he belatedly, *stupidly,* realized she should be far happier about this news than her mood expressed. And since she'd waited so long to tell him about it, he probably wasn't going to be thrilled either. Tiny alarm bells went off inside his head.

"It's not perfect. The pay's not great and hours will be hellish, but I can't be too picky."

"And?" he prompted, waiting for the other shoe to drop.

She lifted her chin. "And it's in Carbondale."

Now he understood her mood. "Please tell me that's a little neighborhood in the suburbs I've just never heard of before."

"No, it's actually the Carbondale."

He chose his words carefully, not liking the sense of déjà vu that settled around this conversation. "Have you accepted it already?"

"No, I told them I needed to think about it, and I'd let

them know by Friday. If I take it, I'd have a week to get settled and start the next Monday."

If she hadn't accepted it, then maybe she was giving him the chance to confirm his last offer. "You don't have to move to Carbondale. I've already told you—"

"That you'd help me out. I know. But I've told *you*—repeatedly—that I'm not looking for a sugar daddy to support me. I want to—I *need* to—accomplish this on my own."

God, she was stubborn. "So you'd rather move to the opposite end of the state instead of accept money from me?"

She shrugged, and his irritation grew. "It's six months, tops."

Here we go again. "What about this?" He indicated the two of them.

That sparked her temper. "*This?* I don't even know what this *is*. It's certainly not enough to give up the opportunity to salvage my career."

Of course. Her precious career was always the most important thing. "It never is, is it?"

"Oh, please. We're going to play *that* song again?" She rolled her eyes at him. "Grow up, Devin. Not everything can be about you. Some things have to be about me, you know? It's six months. Nothing can ever come of *this* if you can't handle six freakin' months." Megan swung her legs off the couch and stood staring down at him. "Just once it would be nice if you could think for a moment beyond your life and your convenience. I put up with a hell of a lot more than six months in Carbondale for you and your career. Moving across the state, switching schools, delaying my graduation because all my credits wouldn't transfer…"

He'd heard this all before, and now she wasn't the only

one getting angry. "Yeah, and nothing was going to stand between you and your career. So you left."

"Damn it, Dev. I'm not asking *you* to move to Carbondale."

Of course not. "Good."

She made a face, but otherwise ignored his comment. "All I'm asking for is your support. Maybe a little cooperation. Just a little inkling that getting involved with you again isn't setting myself up for another crash. I had to choose last time—"

"And you chose your job then, too."

"Because you weren't willing to look for ways to compromise so we could both be happy."

"Compromise?" He snorted. "My choice was Albany or nothing."

Her jaw dropped. "That's not true and you know it."

"Really, Megan? Exactly where did I—or us, for that matter—rank on your list? Couldn't have been very high."

"Don't even *try* to—"

"Oh, I tried. Back then *and* now. I kind of hoped your priority list might have changed a little. Guess I was wrong."

"And I thought *you'd* changed. That you'd try to understand how grown-ups act in a relationship. An *equal* relationship." She tilted her head in that way that annoyed him. "Guess we were both wrong."

He'd been fooling himself that she'd changed. That she'd lost her tunnel vision and was willing to value something more than her job. Like maybe him, for once. But no. They were right back where they'd ended last time. "You got that right."

Megan took a deep breath and her eyes narrowed. "You know, let's just forget it."

"Forget what?"

"All of it. Everything that's happened since I made the mistake of getting anywhere near you again. You go back to your fabulous life and I'll see if I can salvage anything of mine. In Carbondale."

He'd fallen into a time warp. She was walking out on him *again*. At least this time it had happened before he'd gotten all wrapped up in her like a lovesick fool. "If that's what you want, Megan, so be it."

So be it. The same words he'd used when she said she was leaving him last time. His jaw was even set at the same angle and his eyes held the same bitter coldness. Talk about déjà vu. She was twenty-two again, and her heart felt as if it had been slashed with a rusty blade. How could it hurt like this a second time? Had her heart forgotten it had been seven years? Had she just been fooling herself all this time that she was over him? As Devin stared at her, the twitching muscle in his jaw showing his anger, the pain in her chest spread until it was hard to breathe.

She swallowed hard and spoke carefully to keep her voice from shaking. "I'm so glad we had this conversation, Devin. It's nice to know for sure absolutely nothing has changed between us." The pang that shot through her emphasized the underlying truth of that statement. Oh, yeah. She'd been fooling herself. And doing a damn fine job of it until now.

She'd thought about this—Devin, the job in Carbondale, her, her career—from every angle possible the past couple of days. Obviously she'd managed to ignore the great big question right in front of her.

She had her answer now, though.

And she knew what she needed to do.

* * *

"And you just walked out? No more discussion?" Julie's jaw had been hanging open for most of this conversation, but when she did manage to get it working, Megan didn't like the questions. Julie was supposedly there to help her pack, but any packing on her part had come to a screeching halt as soon as Megan started relaying the showdown at Devin's.

"What more was there to discuss? Devin doesn't want me to take this job, even though it's the only way I'll get to finish something that's *very* important to me. It's so selfish of him." She closed the box of glassware and strapped tape across the top. Thankfully, she didn't own a lot of stuff, and anything she didn't absolutely need, Julie had offered to store at her place while she was gone. "Last time around, I supported his goals, and he didn't support mine. I expected better this time."

"May I point out that you didn't really give him a chance?"

Megan sat back on her heels. "I think I did. Devin sees this as a black-and-white issue. Either I stay or I go. No middle ground. I'm not playing that game again."

"Look, I totally agree that Devin is being a bit of a schmuck, and personally I'd love to put him on a spit and slow roast him over hot coals for putting you through all of this. But honey…" Julie's mouth twisted. "I think you're being a bit irrational."

"And I don't think I asked you."

"Someone's testy." Julie shook her head in censure.

"Wouldn't you be? I've had a rough couple of weeks, and I've earned my testiness. My whole life has been turned upside down."

"And Devin's hasn't?"

"Maybe, but not as much as mine. *He* has a successful law practice, a hit radio show and a bestselling book. The poor dear isn't exactly suffering from a little bad press caused by his ex-wife. I, on the other hand…" She sighed and rubbed her temples, trying to release the building tension. "I don't think it's too much to ask, but Devin acts like any ambition I have is some kind of direct slap to him."

Julie tsked. "Sorry, honey, but that sounds like old baggage and self-pity talking."

The barb stung. "You're not a very good counselor, you know," she grumbled.

Unrepentant, Julie smirked at her. "You get handholding and 'how does that make you feel?' when you pay for it. Since this is friendly—and free—girl talk, I'm allowed to tell you when you simply have your panties in a twist."

Megan couldn't believe her ears. "You're really telling me to just get over it?"

"Hmm, maybe not get over it, but definitely grow up and act like a big girl."

It was Megan's turn to go slack jawed. "And to think I'm the one looking for a job. You're the worst counselor I've ever met. I'm calling Dr. Weiss."

Julie waved away the criticism. "But I'm a good friend, honey. I know you want this to be a Feel My Pain conversation—and I do, honestly, I do—but surely you know that you're not thinking clearly."

Another sting. "So since this is girl talk and not actual counseling, tell me what you think I should do."

"You know what you should do."

Of course I do. "Yeah."

"Then call Devin. Apologize for acting like a child and clearly tell him what you want. Give him the opportunity to act like an adult, and maybe you two can work this out." Julie raised an eyebrow at her. "You *do* know what you want, right?"

"I know what I don't want," Megan mumbled, feeling a little sick inside.

"No wonder you two are flailing all over the place. Here's my unsolicited take on the situation. You two got divorced when some really good counseling would have been a better option. Then things go crazy, and you two are thrown back together again. Unsolved problems, emotions not laid to rest, some hormones and you're all messed up again. Am I right?"

The muscles in her stomach clenched around the rock settled there, but she nodded.

"But you know better now. You've worked with couples who were far worse off than you two are and straightened them out. There's nothing here that's unfixable if you're *both* willing to work on it." She cleared her throat. "Solely in my opinion as the world's worst counselor."

"But the bestest friend." Megan thought for a minute. "Do you really think Dev and I can—could, maybe—make this work this time?"

"It'll be tough, but I don't think it's unrealistic to try. And at this point, do you have anything to lose?"

Yeah, I do. Megan grasped for one last lifeline. "If I were your client—a paying client," she amended, "what would you say?"

"I'd recommend some honest conversation about expectations, maybe with a counselor present to assist in keeping you both on topic.... You know the drill, Megan. This is pretty basic stuff."

"I know. No wonder Dr. Weiss fired me. I suck."

"Nah." Julie patted her shoulder. "You're just in the middle of it. Where's Devin now?"

Megan looked at her watch. "Seven-fifteen on a Wednesday night... The studio. I guess I could call him after the show."

"Excellent plan." Julie swung her legs off the couch and slid her feet into her shoes. "I will get out of your way. You should shower and put on something pretty." She eyeballed Megan's battered shorts and ratty T-shirt and frowned. "Or at least presentable. Invite him over tonight and work this out. Like adults."

Megan considered the possibilities. The little spark of hope caused by Julie's pep talk began to glow and grow and relax the painfully clenched muscles in her stomach. "Thanks, Jules."

"You're welcome." Julie picked up her purse and headed for the door. "Call me tomorrow and let me know how it goes. I'll get the spit and fire pit ready, just in case. Good luck, honey." She winked. "My bill will be in the mail."

Once the door closed behind Julie, Megan reached over and turned on her stereo. Devin's voice filled the room, causing little tingles to dance across her skin. Now she didn't want to wait until after the show. She couldn't call the listener line for this, and Dev wouldn't answer his cell while he was on the air, but she could send him a text asking him to call during the break or once he finished. Maybe an email would be better?

The more she thought about it, the more excited and impatient she became. She could be at the studio before the show ended. She could wait outside until he was off the air....

The mention of her name cut through her buzzing thoughts and she froze. She'd been caught in the sound of his voice and ignored the words. But hearing the clipped "Megan" narrowed her focus. She turned up the volume.

"...and I'm telling you it's not worth it. You and your ex are exes for a reason. It's easy sometimes to forget that, maybe even get caught up in the good ol' days, but the truth of the situation never goes away."

"But," the female caller interrupted, "you and Dr. Megan seemed to be—"

Dev's bitter laugh pained her. "See, there's the proof that anyone—it doesn't matter that they know better—can get caught in that trap. Temporary insanity can affect even the best of us."

Her knees felt a little weak.

"My ex swears he's changed, and he really does seem to be different now."

"People don't really change." Devin turned sarcastic. "They tell themselves that, and they'll tell you that, but don't believe it. The truth is that people—at their core—can't change."

In any other situation, Megan would challenge that statement, but the sick feeling in her stomach outweighed any professional outrage.

"Learn from my mistake, folks. It was certainly public enough." He laughed. "Seriously, though, that's the danger of exes. Megan and I had a good run for a while when we were kids, but we shouldn't have gotten married in the first place. I felt sorry for her when the publicity from the book caused her problems—"

The sick feeling started to turn and churn as her anger began to rise.

"—and I let that plus the 'everything old is new again' idea mess with my head. Yeah, hooking up with your ex is fun and exciting for a little while, but nothing good will come of it. That's stupid thinking, folks, and we've talked about stupid thinking on this show dozens of times. Stupid thinking causes you to lose the house *and* the car."

Stupid thinking, indeed. Seems I'm guilty of that.

The caller tried to plead her case. "But sometimes, when we're together, it just seems so right and meant to be."

She didn't think Devin's voice could turn any nastier, but it did. "You mean you're sleeping with your ex again."

"Well..."

"That really *is* stupid. I don't care how good your ex is in bed—and honestly, half the time the reality isn't going to be as good as the memory anyway."

A cold anger slithered down Megan's spine.

"Look, caller, I know I broke one of my top ten rules, and that probably confused a lot of you. But let's just look at this as a good lesson for everyone. We're all susceptible to the heat of an old flame—including me. And while I don't recommend anyone get mixed up with their exes again, if you are—or are looking at your ex and wondering if you should—accept that you made a stupid mistake and run for the hills, folks. Cut your losses."

She wanted to throw something at the speakers. She wanted to smack herself for her stupidity. *I am an idiot.* She shouldn't have let Julie talk her out of her original plan, even for a minute. She'd been right all along.

"You're right, Devin. Thanks."

"You're welcome, caller. We're going to take a short break, and when we come back, we're going to talk more about exes and when you should file for a modification to your original divorce agreement. I'm Devin Kenney, and I'm here to help you Cover Your Assets."

I may be an idiot, but Dev's a jerk. "Way to cover your butt with your listeners by throwing me under the bus, Dev," she said to the radio.

Her earlier excitement had been replaced by indignation and strengthened resolve. She was going to use this as a learning experience and a stepping stone. She'd go into exile in Carbondale, but she'd be back in Chicago soon enough. And when she did return…

Oh, she probably wouldn't be able to do much to Dev—at least nothing on a scale of what he'd done to her recently—but she wouldn't have her hands tied the way she did now.

She'd been right. Dev wasn't good for her—not then, and not now.

So be it.

CHAPTER ELEVEN

AFTER WEEKS OF HEARING nothing but Megan this and Megan that—as well as having Megan in his life and bed again—the absence of all things Megan seemed very strange to Devin. With Megan gone there was little to feed the media circus, and when combined with a local politician's breaking sex scandal, Megan was off the city's radar completely. Her fifteen minutes were finally over.

His life went back to what would be considered normal for him: days at his practice, three shows a week and the occasional appearance for either the show or the book. But even the book's hoopla was dying down now as an organic-gardening-as-spiritual-self-help book made its rise up the lists.

But back to normal felt wrong somehow. It was disturbing because everything was exactly as it should be, yet it all felt hollow and empty. He was getting testy and short-tempered with his callers, even taking one to task on air for being superficial and greedy. *That* hadn't gone over well. He could trace his reaction and lecture right back to Megan—in fact, he might have quoted her at least once—so he held her responsible for his discontent.

The one bright spot in his life—the only thing really holding his interest at the moment—was his involvement with the student's case, which had now almost taken on a life of its own. That involvement had been met with skepticism at first—after all, Devin had staked his professional claim as a divorce attorney, not a constitutional one—but he soon had the skeptics eating crow. That was exhilarating, except he had no one to share the thrill with.

Megan might have accused him of screwing up her life, but he wasn't exactly lovin' his right now either. They were even.

But that didn't make him feel better.

The only person more unhappy than Devin at the moment was Manny, a fact he reminded Devin of constantly. Like now. Devin had Manny on speaker phone, listening with only half an ear while he went through his email in-box.

"That organic-gardening girl is knocking you off the lists."

"I'm still at number eight. I'm hardly toiling in obscurity."

"We need to get you back out there meeting the people and making the papers."

"I don't have time for that right now. This case is taking up what free time I have."

"And that's my point. Pro bono do-gooding doesn't pay the bills." He could almost hear Manny's pout.

At least Manny was consistent. Money talked. "Loan sharks on your case, Manny?"

"Plus, it's even less interesting than it is profitable."

"We are in a sorry state in this country when the denial of a citizen's constitutional rights is considered uninteresting. I thought you could spin anything into headlines."

"That is beyond even my abilities, Devin. Folks aren't interested, and I can't make them be. I'm rather hoping you have another ex-wife tucked away somewhere."

"Dear God, no. One is plenty." The horror in his voice was genuine, as was the pang that shot through him.

"Come on, Devin, give me something meaty to work with."

"The Fourteenth Amendment is pretty enigmatic. Lots of meatiness."

Manny groaned. "You're trying to kill me, right? What say we call Dr. Megan up and see if she's interested in—"

"No."

"When you two are at each other's throats, you're golden. I think a regular He Said–She Said night might be a sellable idea. Maybe just once a week. What do you think?"

"No."

"Can I at least see if Megan is interested?"

"No." *So much for not hearing Megan's name every five minutes.* "End of discussion."

"Fine." Manny sighed dramatically. "Would you be interested in participating in a bachelor auction?"

A bachelor auction? "You really shouldn't drink early in the day, Manny. It's affecting your judgment. Call me when you're sober. Bye."

Manny was still sputtering when Devin disconnected the call. That brought a little smile to Devin's face. For some sick reason, he got a kick out of needling Manny.

Mostly because it was so easy to do. Manny was acting as if the world was ending just because Devin didn't want to renew his contract for *Cover Your Assets.* At least not in its current incarnation. It took up a lot of his time, and honestly, the pessimism was getting to him. If Manny wanted to continue as his agent, he needed to start thinking outside the box.

"Mr. Kenney." His receptionist buzzed in, interrupting

his thoughts. "Dr. Julie Moss is here with a delivery for you."

Julie Moss. She was one of Megan's friends. This was the closest thing to contact he'd had since Megan had stormed out of his place three weeks ago. His first worry—that Megan was sick or hurt—was relieved by the mention of a delivery. Maybe the delivery was a peace offering of sorts? No, he wasn't that lucky. But there was only one way to find out for sure. "You can send her in."

"Um, okay."

It was a strange response from his normally very professional employee, and he wondered if this Julie person was crazy or something. He got his answer when a woman opened his door, nodded a greeting, then held the door open for a man carrying a table.

The coffee table he'd given Megan.

The man set the table down with a grunt of relief, then extended his hand. "Nate Adams. I worked with Megan at the Weiss Clinic."

"And I'm Julie Moss."

Nate seemed friendly enough, but Julie's mouth pulled into a disapproving frown. This was going to be interesting. "Megan mentioned you both."

"Good." Julie replied tersely. "So you can assume she mentioned you to us as well, and we can skip over all the niceties."

Blatant hostility. As a friend of Megan's, he didn't blame her. "What can I—"

"We're just returning the table. I'd have brought it sooner, but I needed Nate's help. It's heavier than it looks."

"Indeed."

Julie cleared her throat. "So Megan asked me to return this to you, and now I have. We'll go, and you can get back to your big, important, famous life."

Sarcasm to go with the hostility. Julie was definitely on Megan's team.

He almost asked why Megan hadn't taken the table with her, but decided against it. "I haven't heard from her since she left." Ignoring Julie's derisive snort, he directed his comment at Nate. "How's she doing?"

The younger man looked distinctly uncomfortable. "Um, fine, I guess. I really don't talk to her that much, you know." He cut his eyes at Julie, as if she would jump in with an answer.

Julie was currently eyeballing him as if he was something she'd found stuck to her shoe, so the chances of any good information on Megan coming from that source seemed slim at best.

In the ensuing silence Nate cleared his throat. "Megan's in Carbondale. Working. Doing great stuff at their clinic. Or so I hear…"

"Good for her."

"Yes, good for her," Julie interrupted. "She's doing quite well in Carbondale. No thanks to you at all." Julie turned to the other man with a false smile. "Nate, could you wait for me in the lobby? I need to talk to Mr. Kenney for a minute."

Profound relief crossed the young man's face. "Of course. Nice meeting you." He beat a hasty retreat, closing the door behind him.

Julie's smile faded when she turned back to him. "Let's cut to the chase."

He leaned against his desk and crossed his arms over his chest. "By all means."

"I don't like you."

"Obviously."

"In fact, I think you're a bit of a jerk. But, in your defense, Megan hasn't exactly been firing on all cylinders lately, so part of that might be a simple reaction to her irrational behavior. Since you're mostly to blame for that behavior, though, you're still a jerk."

"Is there a point you'd like to make, Dr. Moss, or do you just expect me to stand here and allow you to continue to insult me in my own office?"

"As delightful as that sounds, I know that's not likely to happen. Granted, Megan hasn't been the poster child of mental health recently, but I was actually on your side."

"You'll pardon me if I find that difficult to believe."

"I was at first. I even argued on your behalf. Told her how irrational she was being, and we had a major breakthrough."

That would have been after *Megan left me. For the second time. Interesting.*

"Of course, then you went and threw her under the bus on your show."

Guilt nagged at him. He'd been hurt and lashed out. It didn't make anything less true, but the execution had lacked finesse.

"After that," Julie continued, ice dripping off her words, "I couldn't get her out of town fast enough. Hence me being stuck with this table in my living room where I've been tripping over it for the last couple of weeks."

A slightly guilty conscience didn't require him to listen to more of this. "And now you've done your job." He walked to the door and opened it. "Thank you, Dr. Moss."

Julie opened her mouth as if she wanted to say more, then closed it with a snap. "You're welcome, Mr. Kenney."

As she passed him, though, she stopped and eyed him from head to toe as if she was sizing him up for a fight. "Know, however, that Megan does plan to come back to Chicago. And if she's still after your blood then, I won't talk her down."

"Why do I get the feeling you'll drive the getaway car?"

Julie shrugged. "Whatever she needs." With a toss of her hair, she disappeared down the hall.

Devin closed his door and went back to his desk. Between Megan and her friend Julie, he had serious doubts about the relative sanity of so-called mental-health professionals. Craziness seemed to be a prerequisite for the job.

At least at one point, someone—other than him—had been trying to convince Megan she was overreacting. He could take a small bit of satisfaction in that.

However small. And cold.

But Julie's words about Megan being out for blood shocked him more than he wanted to admit. That side of Megan was new. Along with that backbone she'd grown in the past few years, she'd learned to carry a grudge, as well. She wasn't the same Megan he used to know, that was for sure.

That thought stopped him. Megan *wasn't* the same. She was a different person. He'd accepted and appreciated her new confidence but not that she wanted to be treated as an equal, instead of being taken care of. How had he managed to miss that?

He hadn't missed it; he'd ignored it. She'd told him directly numerous times and it hadn't sunk in. Seemed he was as hardheaded as Megan accused him of being. When faced with the possibility of reconciliation, he'd expected them to pretty much pick up where they'd left off—at least where they'd been before he asked her to move to Chicago. He'd enjoyed her new backbone and attitude, but hadn't processed the fact that it meant she wasn't the Megan he used to know.

Insanity was doing the same thing over again and expecting a different result. He'd expected something different and then been surprised when he'd gotten the exact result as last time: Megan gone.

Either the crazy was contagious or he deserved every insult Megan hurled his way.

And it was pretty clear he wasn't crazy.

The only real question was whether or not there was anything left to salvage out of this mess.

Thursday was becoming Megan's least favorite day. There was a sound reason she didn't like a client list packed full of substance abusers, and Thursday was the day she had groups back-to-back-to-back. The host of other problems the substance abuse caused—with spouses, children, the law—was both depressing and demoralizing. Depressing because she got so tired of seeing families torn apart over it, and demoralizing because there was often so little she could do to really help. Most of the time the damage was done and she was just trying to help pick up the pieces. Not every counselor was made to counsel every kind of client. She knew that.

But it was tougher than usual right now. Rationally, she knew her feelings were being compounded by the sad state of her personal life. She didn't really have much of one to speak of.

She'd been so busy at the clinic since she arrived she hadn't had time to make any friends or even explore the town. What little free time she had, she was usually so exhausted or brain dead all she wanted to do was watch TV. She talked to her mom, and Julie called to keep her up-to-date on things in Chicago, but otherwise...

She was bored. She was lonely.

And she was pregnant.

It seemed there really was no end to the upheaval and chaos Devin Kenney could bring to her life.

Moving here hadn't gotten Dev off her mind; no matter how much she tried to focus on her job and lose herself in the work, he was always there, poking around the edges of her concentration. And if that wasn't enough, he seemed to haunt her dreams, leaving her feeling empty and frustrated in the mornings.

In fact, she'd almost ignored the fact she'd missed her period, assuming it was just stress and obsession over Dev manifesting in physical ways. How wrong she was.

She couldn't get Dev out of her mind, and now she was carrying his baby in her body, as well. His hold on her was permanent now.

Like it wasn't already.

They'd talked about having kids. Even discussed some baby names, although to no one's surprise, they'd never managed to come to an agreement.

Did the universe hate her? After falling in love with Devin, spending seven years trying to get over him, then falling in love with him again only to lose him again, she got pregnant with his child *now?*

It was enough to make her want to pull her hair out.

At least she was being honest with herself. She was in love with Devin again and realizing she'd probably never really gotten over him in the first place. Having that under-standing would help her get through this—even if it didn't make it hurt any less.

And this hurt a lot. No amount of self-therapy could help. Even having Julie admit she'd been wrong and come fully onto her side didn't help. The misery ran deep.

Somehow, amazingly enough, this time seemed to hurt more than last time. Even though she was fueled by the same righteous indignation, it didn't provide much solace this time. Being right in principle had helped before, but now it was cold comfort—and not even much of that, since she wasn't even sure she was right in principle now. Or that she cared who was right or wrong in the first place.

She was completely miserable, and the only thing that kept her from driving back to Chicago to tell Devin that was the knowledge—in his own words—that he considered her a mistake.

That cut to the quick.

She wondered how long it would take for the pain to lessen enough for her to talk to Devin without admitting she'd been stupid and wrong and begging for another chance. She'd have to talk to him eventually. She had to tell him about the baby. This wasn't the kind of thing she could just keep to herself. It wouldn't be fair to Devin or the baby—or her, either. She'd just have to suck it up and deal.

Eventually. Right now she wanted to wallow. It was easier. Going to bed and getting today over with sounded like the best plan ever. She could wallow herself to sleep.

Julie's ring tone blared on the end table behind her. Without opening her eyes she reached for her phone.

"What's up, Ju—"

"Turn on your radio. *Now.*"

The urgency in Julie's voice spurred her into action even as she sputtered questions. "Why? What's going on?"

"It's Devin. You've got to hear this."

"Dev's show isn't on tonight," she argued even as she searched for the channel.

"He's doing an interview with Bruce Malaney and now they're talking about *you.*"

Megan's heart crawled into her throat. Bruce Malaney shared his philosophy of anything-for-ratings with Kate and her ilk. Was there no end to this? The static finally cleared, and she turned the volume up.

Devin's voice came out of the speakers and curled through her as he spoke. At least he didn't sound angry. "...not really speaking to each other right now, as I'm sure you can imagine, but I hear she's doing well."

"That info came from me," Julie said.

"Shh! I can't hear."

"Of course," Bruce said, "your recent relationship with her was major news."

Dev laughed. "I'm not sure I'd use the word *news*, but it was something people took an interest in. I'm feeling more sympathy for celebrities and their relationships now, though, that's for sure."

Bruce and his listeners might not catch the edge to Devin's voice, but Megan heard it loud and clear.

"People are speculating that Megan Lowe might be indirectly or directly responsible for ending your show."

What? "Julie, what's this about Devin's show?" Megan asked.

"They talked about that earlier." Julie spoke quickly. "*Cover Your Assets* is being overhauled somehow. Devin was cagey about what it would be when it returned...."

Megan couldn't listen to Julie and Devin both. "Shh."

"The only thing Megan is responsible for," Devin said, "is opening my eyes to details I've been missing, both personally and professionally. In its current format, *Cover Your Assets* has really outlived its original purpose. I've found out you can't really help people with quick, pithy sound bites during a ten-minute radio conversation."

Megan bit her lip in disbelief.

"So what is next for you, Devin?" Bruce asked. "You evaded the question earlier, so I'm going to pin you down now."

Devin took a deep breath. "I don't want to get stuck in a rut. This situation with Megan showed me I was headed there. People fear change, but change opens doors and adds possibilities. I'm going to explore some possibilities."

Megan was feeling light-headed and realized it was because she was holding her breath. Somehow, though, she couldn't get her lungs working properly.

Bruce laughed. "Sounds like your next book will be a self-help tome."

"I think the last few weeks have proven beyond a shadow of a doubt that I'm the last person who should be handing out advice to people on how to manage their lives. I'll leave that to the experts like Megan."

"Megan, did you hear that?" Julie asked breathlessly, but Megan couldn't find her voice through her shock. "Megan?"

"We're going to take a short break. We'll be back with more from divorce expert and newly minted legal crusader Devin Kenney in a few minutes. I'm Bruce Malaney and this is *Clear the Air.*"

Megan couldn't believe her ears. There was no way she'd heard that right. Wishful thinking obviously led to auditory hallucinations. Or maybe early pregnancy had her hearing what she wanted to hear. Because if what Dev had just said was real...

"Megan!" Julie's shout finally broke through, and Megan slapped the volume down as the show went to commercial.

"I'm here. Did you hear what I just heard?"

"Oh, my God, *yes.* That was practically a public apology. Not to mention a hell of a shout-out to the counseling prowess of Dr. Megan."

"So you don't think I'm reading too much into that."

"Read *more* into it, honey. There's no way Devin could

be sure you were listening, so that wasn't for your benefit. You need to call him."

"And say what?"

"Start with 'I'm sorry for being psycho' and go from there."

Now that the paralysis had passed, Megan felt full of restless energy. She hauled herself to her feet and started to pace. "I have his cell. I could call him tonight after the show. Apologize. See if any of that was an olive branch."

"Excellent idea."

"But what if it's not? What if he's just putting a good face on all this for the sake of the masses? Like you said, there's no way he could guarantee I'd be listening tonight."

"You won't know until you talk to him, now, will you?"

She needed to find out. Especially considering… She laid a hand on her stomach. She needed to find out what Dev meant with all of that before she told him about the baby.

And out of nowhere, a little spark of hope flared in the darkness.

Possibilities, indeed. Suddenly there were a whole lot of possibilities to explore, and some of those possibilities now held a golden, promising glow.

"I do need to talk to Devin." *But I need to see his face while I do it.*

"Duh. That's what I've been saying."

"Let me make a few phone calls." Megan was already mentally rearranging her schedule. "Can I crash at your place tonight?"

"You're coming in? Tonight?"

"Yeah. I'll go see Devin in the morning before his show."

"You're a brave girl."

She didn't feel brave. If she was reading the wrong meaning into Dev's words, she would regret it—horribly—tomorrow.

But right now there was the possibility she wouldn't.

Devin had one eye on the clock as he halfheartedly dispensed advice to his listeners. So far, the calls had been pretty evenly split between questions about his announcement that the show would be undergoing some major changes and the news of Hollywood's latest power-couple breakup.

Despite his best attempts to steer the discussion away from the couple's private life, that was exactly what the audience wanted to speculate about. He wasn't going to add fuel to that fire if he could at all help it, so he was trying to shift the focus to prenuptial agreements in general.

Paula-from-Milwaukee seemed awfully distraught for someone who had no real stake in the possible settlement, and he bit back the urge to tell her to seek counseling about her overinvestment in the lives of people she didn't even know. "Paula, I haven't seen their prenup, so I have no idea how it's worded, but California law does not recognize adultery as grounds for divorce."

"But if she's sleeping with her costar…"

Twenty more minutes and this show would be over. He still had a long drive to Carbondale ahead of him and possibly a long night if Megan decided to be stubborn or nurse her grudge. His patience was wearing thin, and he motioned to Mike, Kate's replacement, that this call needed to be wrapped up. "Let's not speculate about the private lives of others, okay? I think the point we need to take away from this is that prenuptial agreements aren't always ironclad."

Mike was quick on the draw. "Let's find a new caller

and see what other topics are out there. I personally would like to talk about that case in Michigan where the couple is fighting over custody of the parrot, but…"

Sixteen minutes left. "Pick a caller, Mike."

"Here's a lady who's been waiting patiently in the queue for a while now. You're on the air, caller."

"Finally," a voice Devin recognized muttered. "This is Megan, and, um, I'm from Carbondale."

Astonished, Devin looked through the window at Mike, who simply shrugged unhelpfully. After all this time, Megan called his show? What the…?

"Hello? Hello? Did I get disconnected? Damn."

"No, you're on the air, Megan." *Treat her like you would any other caller.* "Do you have a question or a comment?"

"Both, actually. I heard your interview last night." She laughed, but it lacked any real humor. "Since I'm not exactly a regular listener, most of that was news to me."

"And?" he prompted.

"So my question is about possibilities. Like the ones you mentioned last night."

Devin tried to remember exactly what he'd said.

"I'm usually a big fan of possibilities, and in my line of work I kinda have to be, but recently I've had some trouble with the idea."

"That's the thing about possibilities. Once you start questioning them, you start cutting off options."

"Yes, Devin, I know that," Megan snapped, but then seemed to remember where she was. "I mean—" she tried again with a different tone "—how do you know when you've totally crossed a possibility off your list?"

Outside the booth's main window, a crowd was gathering. Staff had come out of their cubicles to gather around the booth and its speaker. In his booth, Mike moved at high speed between phone and computer, looking as if he was under siege. A glance at his own computer screen told him why: Mike *was*.

The call lines were lit up like a Christmas tree and the hold queue had reached new lengths. Comments were already getting posted on his website bulletin board under a brand-new thread titled "Dr. Megan is back—now!"

This is not how I planned to have a conversation with Megan today. He was still forming his plan of attack and had rather counted on the ride to southern Illinois to flesh it out. But what he said here could have massive repercussions later tonight. "I'm not sure I'm the right person to come to with that question, Megan. I specialize in divorce, not—"

"No, you're the right person. I'm not using a generic 'you' here in my question. I mean how do you, Devin Kenney, decide a possibility has been totally removed from the list?"

The booth might have been soundproof, but he could still see the crowd outside take a collective breath, even if he couldn't hear it. Everything seemed to freeze.

"Megan, I'm not sure this is the right forum—"

"I'm sorry, Dev. I was wrong and I'm sorry and I miss you and I'd really like to talk about possibilities." She paused, and her voice seemed to shrink. "If you're still willing, that is."

Devin swallowed hard, unsure if he'd heard her right. "Megan—"

Mike's voice came through his headphones. "Damn, they just crashed the server. Your site's down."

Devin ignored him. "We need to talk, but this probably isn't the best venue."

"God, you're right. I'm sorry, Dev. I'll wait down here until you're done."

Down here? "Megan, where are you?"

"The lobby on fourteen. The security guard wouldn't let me up and the receptionist—"

"Stay there." He was on his feet and taking off his headphones before the words were fully out of his mouth. "Go to commercial," he barked at Mike, who nodded, his eyes wide. Outside the booth he passed his slack-jawed audience without pausing on his way to the stairwell.

When he opened the door to the fourteenth-floor lobby, Megan was easy to spot. She stood in the middle of the room with half a dozen people staring wordlessly at her, keeping a safe distance as if she was a ticking time bomb. When she spied him, a small smile tried to form, then faded.

Every eye in the room turned to him at that moment, and he froze, unsure of what to do next.

Dev looked much like the wrath of God bearing down on her, and Megan worried she'd handled this situation all wrong. Devin stopped about five feet from her and those rich brown eyes nearly stared her into the ground.

"Hi, Dev," she said feeling lame and embarrassed at the same time.

"What are you doing here?"

"I tried calling you all morning, but you never answered and you never called me back...."

"You're not the only one who can ignore a telephone after an interview draws attention."

"And then the receptionist was supposed to tell you I was here and I just couldn't wait any longer. So I called. I didn't mean to raise a ruckus on your show. I'm sorry about that, too. Jeez, can I just do a blanket apology for everything and start over?"

For the first time she could ever remember, Dev seemed shocked speechless. Finally he managed, "What?"

Their audience was now staring openly, avidly hanging on every word. Somewhere a phone rang, unanswered. She could feel heat creeping up her neck. "Umm... Well..."

Dev looked at the crowd, then reached for her hand. "Come on."

She followed him without question as he led her back into the stairwell. The gray walls echoed the sound of the door closing, and she turned to find Dev leaning against it. *Now or never.* "Dev, I'm sorry about everything. You were right about—"

Devin moved like a streak of lightning, pinning her against the wall before she realized it. A second later his mouth landed on hers in a kiss that stole her breath and made her scalp tingle in delight.

She was left gasping when he finally broke away and ran a hand over her hair. "I'll accept your apology if you'll accept mine."

"Yours?"

"You were right about a few things, too. In fact, I was headed to Carbondale after the show to tell you exactly that."

Hope kindled in her chest. "You were?"

"I was being a selfish jerk. Again."

"Well, I wasn't doing much better," she admitted.

"See, we're meant to be together. No one else would put up with us."

"About Carbondale, though..."

"As you said, it's six months, maybe less. We'll work it out. You tell me what you need, and I'll do my part."

That was too easy. "Just like that?"

"Just like that."

Her world clicked into place. Maybe it was that easy. "I love you, Dev. I don't think I ever stopped."

"Good. Because I know I never stopped loving you." Dev's smile made her heart melt into a warm puddle. She wrapped her arms around his neck and pulled him close for another kiss. As the kiss deepened, Dev pressed her back against the cinder block wall. She threaded her fingers through his hair and let him catch her happy sigh in his mouth. Then his lips moved to her neck....

The loud crash of the door above opening forcefully into the wall caused her to jump. Devin's flustered producer started down the stairs two at a time before he saw them and skittered to a stop. The shocked look on his face melted into a grin. "Well, this answers one question." He cleared his throat. "Devin, it's a zoo up there. What do you want me to do?"

Devin pressed a kiss to her forehead, but didn't move from his position or even look behind him. "Megan, you remember Mike?"

Feeling a little embarrassed at the position she was currently in, Megan managed to lift her hand and wave her fingers. "Hi, Mike. Sorry about the commotion."

"Hi, Dr. Megan. Glad you're back. Well, Devin?"

"Tell the listeners Devin and Dr. Megan will be back in a few minutes with a—" Dev paused and smiled at her "—big announcement."

Speaking of big announcements...

"Will do." Mike was gone before the words stopped echoing off the walls.

When Devin leaned in for another kiss, she stopped him with a hand on his chest. He changed direction and went for her earlobe. She fought back her shiver at the touch. "Dev, there's something I need to tell you."

"Now?" he murmured against the sensitive skin of her neck.

She debated, but the need to lay everything out on the table won. "Yeah."

Concern was etched on his face as he pulled back and his eyes met hers. "What?"

Cupping her hands under his jaw, she met his eyes steadily. "Before I tell you, though, know that it has *nothing* to do with anything I've just said. I'd be here regardless. I just want you to know everything before we go any further."

She could tell her words worried him. His eyebrows drew together in a V. "What's wrong?"

"Nothing's wrong. At least not to me. I mean, I'm okay—more than okay, actually. It's just…"

"Then quit dancing around the subject and tell me."

She took a deep breath and prayed this happy moment wasn't going to be short-lived because of her announcement. "I'm pregnant."

This time Dev really did seem speechless. In fact, as his jaw dropped, Megan was afraid she'd really stepped in something.

"You're sure?"

"Positive." When Devin didn't say anything, her heart started to crumple in on itself. "Dev? Are you okay?" Devin's frown reversed itself into a smile that caused her stomach to flutter. "I know we'll need to talk about the whole where-I'm-living issue, but—"

He cut her off with another soul-stirring kiss that removed all her doubts. "Like I said earlier, we'll work it out."

Yesterday she wouldn't have believed it, but today she did. It was that simple.

"Marry me."

It was her turn to be shocked nearly speechless. She swallowed hard. "I didn't tell you about the baby to get a proposal."

"And I'm not proposing because of the baby. He's just a bonus."

"It could be a girl," she reminded him.

Dev grinned. "I guess anything is possible." With a sigh, he looked at the stairs and the door above. "Come on," he said, threading his fingers through hers. "Let's go save Mike and tell the listeners the news."

Last month, even contemplating such a thing would have convinced her she was certifiably insane. But things had changed, and, as always, change brought possibilities.

Anything is possible.

Maybe even a happy ending for them.

EPILOGUE

WHEN MEGAN CAME OUT of the bedroom in search of something to drink, she was surprised to find Devin fully dressed as he flipped through the paper. She'd heard him get up and she'd promptly gone back to sleep, but she didn't think she'd snoozed for *that* long. She was sleeping almost as much now as she had in her first trimester. So much for those "bursts of nesting energy" she was supposed to be getting the closer she got to her due date.

He looked up as she waddled in. The deep gold of his tie brought out the color of his eyes, and the starched white shirt contrasted nicely with his dark hair. "Good morning."

"Look at you, all dressed up to impress the judges. You look sexy in a tie, you know."

He pulled at the knot at his throat as if it was uncomfortable. "Rumor has it you have to wear a tie when you appear in front of the State Supreme Court. I sincerely hope it's *not* because the judges find it sexy. That's just too disturbing to think about."

"Doesn't matter. It's still sexy to me." To prove her point, she tugged on the tie until his lips met hers for a good-morning kiss. "Good luck today."

"Thanks, but I don't need luck. I have the Constitution backing me up." Devin reached for something next to his briefcase. "This came for you yesterday. You fell asleep before I could mention it."

The sight of the long white envelope had her heart pumping before she even confirmed the return address as the Department of Professional Regulation. *This is it. Moment of truth.* Her mouth went dry and she refused to take it. "I can't open it. You read it."

"Eight months ago you were positive you'd ace this thing with your eyes closed and your couch tied behind your back."

"That was bravado talking. Now I'm not so cocky about it."

Dev studied the envelope. "I don't even need to open it. Congrats, Meggie."

Aw. "Thanks for the vote of confidence, but…"

He held it out again, an exasperated look on his face. "Read who it's addressed to."

She took the envelope and looked at it. Her heart started to beat double time. She looked again to be sure and read it aloud. "'Dr. Megan Lowe, LCP.'"

"Nice set of letters you got there."

"I did it." She could feel the goofy grin stretching across her face. "I actually did it. Dr. Megan Lowe, Licensed Clinical Psychologist, at your service. How can I serve your mental-health needs today?"

Dev put his arms around her waist—or what was left of it. "Well, you could give me some reassurance."

"My pleasure. Want some positive affirmations?" She looked into the beautiful brown eyes she hoped the baby would inherit and grinned. "Repeat after me. 'I am a great lawyer. I will knock the Supreme Court dead with my arguments today.'"

Dev shook his head. "I was thinking more along the

lines of 'Yes, Dev, I will marry you *before* I give birth to your child.'"

"Yes, Dev, I will marry you before I give birth to your child," she parroted. "Now that I have this—" she shook the envelope "—checked off my to-do list, you can name the date."

"Next week," he challenged.

If he was trying to bluff her, he was in for a big surprise. "Deal. But I can't change my name until it's time to renew my license."

"Fair enough."

"Really?" That was too easy.

"I don't care which name you use professionally—Dr. Lowe, Dr. Kenney, Dr. Megan… Hell, call yourself Dr. Zhivago, for all I care."

She smacked his arm. "Not Dr. Zhivago. Or Dr. Megan. Although it's going to be weird to be Megan Kenney again."

"Weird how?"

"How many times can one person change her name back and forth? It took me forever to get everything switched back to Lowe last time. I was still getting catalogs addressed to Megan Kenney last year."

"Well, whatever you decide, you'll never have to change your name again." He winked. "Or move to Canada."

For someone who'd made a small fortune from being the world's biggest cynic on marriage, Dev had pitched his tent in the other camp pretty quickly. "You really don't have a preference about me changing my name?"

Devin placed a kiss on her forehead. "You can call yourself anything you want. I just want to call you mine."

Tears burned in the corners of her eyes. "That's probably the sweetest thing you've ever said to me." *Great, now this baby is making me all weepy, too.*

Dev looked shocked. "That's very sad. No wonder you divorced me."

"No, I divorced you because I thought you weren't giving me what I needed."

"And now?" he prompted.

She pretended to think on his question, but the answer really didn't require thought, soul-searching, or discussion with a counselor of any sort.

"I couldn't ask for anything more."

Harlequin Presents

Coming Next Month

from **Harlequin Presents®**. Available March 29, 2011.

Coming Next Month

from **Harlequin Presents® EXTRA**. Available April 12, 2011.

REQUEST YOUR
FREE BOOKS!

HARLEQUIN *Presents* ®

2 FREE NOVELS PLUS
2 FREE GIFTS!

PASSION
GUARANTEED
SEDUCTION

YES! Please send me 2 FREE Harlequin Presents® novels and my 2 FREE gifts (gifts are worth about $10). After receiving them, if I don't wish to receive any more books, I can return the shipping statement marked "cancel." If I don't cancel, I will receive 6 brand-new novels every month and be billed just $4.05 per book in the U.S. or $4.74 per book in Canada. That's a saving of at least 15% off the cover price! It's quite a bargain! Shipping and handling is just 50¢ per book.* I understand that accepting the 2 free books and gifts places me under no obligation to buy anything. I can always return a shipment and cancel at any time. Even if I never buy another book, the two free books and gifts are mine to keep forever.

106/306 HDN E5M4

Name   (PLEASE PRINT)

Address   Apt. #

City   State/Prov.   Zip/Postal Code

Signature (if under 18, a parent or guardian must sign)

Mail to the **Harlequin Reader Service:**
IN U.S.A.: P.O. Box 1867, Buffalo, NY 14240-1867
IN CANADA: P.O. Box 609, Fort Erie, Ontario L2A 5X3

Not valid for current subscribers to Harlequin Presents books.

Are you a current subscriber to Harlequin Presents books and want to receive the larger-print edition? Call 1-800-873-8635 today!

* Terms and prices subject to change without notice. Prices do not include applicable taxes. N.Y. residents add applicable sales tax. Canadian residents will be charged applicable provincial taxes and GST. Offer not valid in Quebec. This offer is limited to one order per household. All orders subject to approval. Credit or debit balances in a customer's account(s) may be offset by any other outstanding balance owed by or to the customer. Please allow 4 to 6 weeks for delivery. Offer available while quantities last.

Your Privacy: Harlequin Books is committed to protecting your privacy. Our Privacy Policy is available online at www.eHarlequin.com or upon request from the Reader Service. From time to time we make our lists of customers available to reputable third parties who may have a product or service of interest to you. If you would prefer we not share your name and address, please check here. ☐

Help us get it right—We strive for accurate, respectful and relevant communications. To clarify or modify your communication preferences, visit us at www.ReaderService.com/consumerschoice.

HP10R

*Selene wanted nothing to do with the father of her son,
Alex; but Aristedes had other plans...that included them.*

*Read on for an sneak peek from
THE SARANTOS SECRET BABY by Olivia Gates,
available April 2011, only from Harlequin Desire.*

"You were right to turn my marriage offer down," Aristedes said.

And Selene found her voice at last, found the words that
would not betray the blow he'd dealt her. "Thanks for letting me know. You didn't have to come all the way here,
though. You could have just let it go. I left yesterday with
the understanding that this case is closed."

Before the hot needles behind her eyes could dissolve
into an unforgivable display of stupidity and weakness, she
began to close the door.

The door stopped against an immovable object. His flat palm.

"I can't accept that." His voice was low, leashed.

What did her tormentor mean now? Was he ending one
game only to start another?

She raised eyes as bruised as her self-respect to his,
found nothing there but solemnity and determination.

Before she could voice her confusion, he elaborated. "I
never let anything go unless I'm certain it's unworkable. I
realize I made you an unworkable offer, and that's why I'm
withdrawing it. I'm here to offer something else. A work-
ability study."

She leaned against the door, thankful for its support and
partial shield. "Your son and I are not a business venture
you can test for feasibility."

His gaze grew deeper, made her feel as if he was trying
to delve into her mind, take control of it. "It's actually the

other way around. I'm the one who would be tested."

She shook her head. "Why bother? I know—and *you* know—you're not workable. Not with me."

His spectacular eyebrows lowered over eyes she felt were emitting silver hypnosis. "You're right again. Neither you nor I have any reason to believe that isn't the truth. The only truth. It might be best for both you and Alex to never hear from me again, to forget I exist. But then again, maybe not. I'm only asking for the chance for both of us to find out for certain. You believe I'm unworkable in any personal relationship. I've lived my life based on that belief about myself. I never really had reason to question it. But I have one now. In fact, I have two."

Find out what happens in
THE SARANTOS SECRET BABY by Olivia Gates,
available April 2011, only from Harlequin Desire.

HARLEQUIN® HISTORICAL:
Where love is timeless

USA TODAY
BESTSELLING AUTHOR
MARGARET MOORE
INTRODUCES
Highland Heiress

SUED FOR BREACH OF PROMISE!

No sooner does Lady Moira MacMurdaugh breathe a sigh of relief for avoiding a disastrous marriage to Dunbrachie's answer to Casanova than she is served with a lawsuit! By the very man who saved her from a vicious dog attack, no less: solicitor Gordon McHeath. Torn between loyalty for a friend and this beautiful woman who stirs him to ridiculous distraction, Gordon knows he can't have it both ways....

But when sinister forces threaten to upend Lady Moira's world, Gordon simply can't stand idly by and watch her fall!

Available from Harlequin Historical
April 2011

❧ Harlequin®

A *Romance* FOR EVERY MOOD™

www.eHarlequin.com

HH29638